PANGUR BAN

Other Novels By Mary Stolz

The Explorer of Barkham Street
Cat Walk
What Time of Night Is It?
Go and Catch a Flying Fish
Cider Days
Ferris Wheel
The Edge of Next Year
Lands End
By the Highway Home
A Wonderful, Terrible Time
The Noonday Friends
The Bully of Barkham Street
A Dog on Barkham Street
The Scarecrows and Their Child
Storm in the Night

For Younger Readers

Emmett's Pig
(An I Can Read Book)

PANGUR BAN

by Mary Stolz

illuminations by
Pamela Johnson

An Ursula Nordstrom Book

HARPER & ROW, PUBLISHERS, New York
Cambridge, Philadelphia, San Francisco, St. Louis
London, Singapore, Sydney

Translation of the poem "Pangur Ban" from *Trírech inna n-Én* © 1926 by Robin Flower. Reprinted by permission of Patrick Flower.

Pangur Ban
Copyright © 1988 by Mary Stolz
Typography by Joyce Hopkins
1 2 3 4 5 6 7 8 9 10
First Edition

Library of Congress Cataloging-in-Publication Data
Stolz, Mary, date
    Pangur Ban / Mary Stolz. — 1st ed.
    p.   cm
    Summary: Fifteen-year-old Cormac, longing to fulfill his artistic inclinations, leaves his family farm in ninth-century Ireland and joins a monastery, where he creates an illuminated manuscript to be treasured by generations to come.
    ISBN 0-06-025861-6 : $. ISBN 0-06-025862-4
                         (lib. bdg.) : $
    [1. Ireland—Fiction.   2. Religious life—Fiction.   3. Artists—Fiction.]   I. Title.
PZ7.S875854Pan 1988   87-35049
[Fic]—dc19   CIP
                                                        AC

For Ursula Nordstrom and Mary Griffith
long-known, long-loved

Author's Note

This novel was inspired by the poem "Pangur Ban," a translation by Robin Flower of a manuscript, found in the monastery of St. Paul in Carinthia, dating from approximately the ninth century. The poem itself was written by an anonymous monk on the parchment pages of a missal he was transcribing. The thought of the monk-scribe and his white cat intrigued the author for many years and prompted her to write this story about them.

PART ONE
Ireland, A.D. 813–814

PART ONE

CHAPTER I

ORMAC, SON OF Liam
Brudair, yeoman, heard
his name echo through the woods like a bullock's
bellow. He started nervously, and his pen, a stout
primary feather dropped by a rook, slipped and made
a line where he'd not intended one.

Ready to pack and run in obedience to his father's
angry summons, he stayed a moment, peering at the
accidental line slanting across the field mouse he'd
been drawing. It looked like a weed waving in front of
his mouse, and seemed to give the sketch a touch he
hadn't thought of. A sort of natural air, he decided,
absently selecting another quill, dipping it in his green
ink.

He had fashioned a palette from a wide board,
scooping depressions to hold dyes that he made

himself, extracting juices from cranberries, wild raspberries, from the berries of the blackthorn, the alder, the rowan. He squeezed color from the wild radish, and the petals of buttercups, from sneezeweed that grew in the swampy edges of the peat bogs, from water willow and gentians and wood sorrels and moss.

He was working on one of several sheets of bark stripped from fallen trees, then retted, pounded, dried on stones. With a piece of flint he had drawn the outline of a field mouse, sitting up, head turned a little as if attentive to a sound, a stirring in the grass.

Now he drew a curved stem where the quill had scratched as if guiding itself. Next, of course, was what kind of weed should it be? Ragged robin, maybe— using cranberry mixed with a little water to make it pink.

"Cormac, you gormless calf! When I catch you, you'll wish yourself unborn!"

Tongue caught at the corner of his mouth, Cormac worked on, and though his father's repeated summons rang through the trees he heard it as he heard corncrakes scouring gleaned grain fields, or the bark of a fox somewhere beyond the millpond, or the clatter of a hedgehog passing in the undergrowth a few yards away.

That was, he heard it not at all.

As he attempted to catch his mouse in its setting, Pangur Ban, his white cat, was on a hunt for the real thing. Crouched, tail tip and whiskers quivering, he waited, waited, and waited still—then, haunches briefly wagging, he sprang!

4

Where he landed—no mouse.

Delicately brushing in the petals of ragged robin, Cormac spared part of his attention, smiling at his cat. "You are young at your trade, Pangur Ban, as I at mine. But we will learn."

Pangur, little more than a kitten, would one day get his mouse every time, unless he chose not to, a way that cats had. Cat and mouse, that was the order of things. One to hunt, one to be hunted, one to fail at times, one to escape. All was ordered in the lives of beasts. Mule and bullock to work; sheep, cosseted like babies for their wool and milk, to idle their days away; birds to fly; salmon to leap.

All, all—doing as God intended for them to do.

Only—what about me? Cormac asked himself. Surely God intended for me to be an artist. Why else would it be in me, this need to draw, to squeeze colors from plants, to defy my hard-working, hard-handed, honest, and angry father.

"You know," he said, looking directly at heaven, "I did not set out to be so. It fell upon me when I was not looking at all, and here I am, hiding in the woods, due for the switch when I get home, and is it to be for nothing?"

Clouds were mounting in the western sky, folding over like waves. There was a rumbling behind them, and the rooks were wheeling in circles. Maybe it would rain, and his da would decide not to deliver the apple tribute to castle and abbey this day. He, his father, his sister and brothers had spent the morning in the orchard, picking not their own share, but the tithe.

Now if it should storm, their own portion would be wrinkled windfalls.

Why would a man be a farmer? Because he had no choice. The da and the da and the da of his da had been yeoman farmers all, no more able to say, "I will not," than their bullock could declare he took no pleasure in ceaseless labor and from this out he'd grow wool and be a lazy-living sheep; or a ewe proclaim she was weary of lambing and proposed to grow feathers and fly up like a lark or a lapwing.

But surely, now and then, a man—well, a boy—could say, *"I will not,"* and turn his back on the farm?

He did not think it likely.

He would not learn to fly like a bird, leap like a salmon, give wool like a ram. Neither would he become an artist, the unlettered, ignorant, rather lazy farmer's son that he was.

Sighing, he washed his quill in a bit of broken crockery he used for holding water. He wrapped the board of inks carefully, so as not to spill them, in an old piece of cowhide, smooth side in. His mother had given it him. Had *stolen* it for him.

He stowed it, his quills, the piece of bark on which he was drawing the mouse, deep in a badger set he used for a hiding place. Pulling branches across the opening to conceal it, he put Pangur Ban on his shoulder and started for home, his father, and his deserved punishment.

Trudging along the cowpath, he called himself first an oaf, then an artist, feeling he was both.

"Where's that cowhide that I had in the barn?" Liam Brudair had demanded one morning, glaring at his children, his mother, his wife, then fixing the mightiest glare on Cormac. "I'll have an answer, or no one eats this day."

"How have an answer," said his wife. My mother, Cormac reminded himself now, putting her soul in peril through the sin of lying for me. "How answer," she had asked her husband, "when no one's to know what's become of it at all ... filched, perhaps, by some wandering beggar, some escaped slave—God give him the means to freedom. You wouldn't stint a poor soul the way of keeping warm, the hard weather coming on and he with no bed or roof or family to turn to—the way we in the house are so blessed—"

The farmer had studied his wife's open, guileless face, listened to her words of pity for this homeless wretch who'd made off with his cowhide, and lifted his hands in surrender.

"If," he said, "I were not caught in your web, helpless as any fly, Megeen, things would be different under this rooftree, let me tell you."

"I know that," she said softly. "But deep down, are you not glad of it, to be here in my web, Liam Brudair?"

"I'd have to dig a long sight down before I'd be glad of losing my cowhide," he muttered.

Cormac, with a faint urge to confess, had caught his mother's eye, and subsided guiltily. After all, he and his mother confessed their misdeeds to Father

7

Maher at the abbey, which should put things right with everyone but his father.

Swinging along through the woods, able to put punishment out of mind until actually enduring it, Cormac thought about the brothers of the abbey, high on their broad tableland overlooking the sea.

He knew that they labored daylong, like farmers of the glen. Knew, too, that life in the abbey was severe, silent, rigid. That to be accepted was not easy of achievement. That once there a man—a boy—turned his back on the world of family and friends.

But there was peace and prayer and order on that rocky escarpment. When he and his mother and the other children climbed the rock steps to the lay part of the church for Mass, confession, communion, that ordered peace was like a gentle hand on his brow, a draught of honey easing his throat.

But above all else for Cormac was this—within the walls of the abbey on the high hill, there was learning.

He stopped, crossing his arms on his chest, closing his eyes, as at a vision too radiant for direct gazing.

Some of those monks wrote books.

They lettered, on parchment, on vellum, gospels, missals, classical myths in Latin, in Irish, in Greek. They were blessed above all other creatures on earth.

They knew reading.

They could write.

Standing on the cowpath, alone with his cat, Cormac felt a familiar, scalding envy. Envy. Yet another sin. A breaking of the tenth commandment.

He could no more prevent it than order his lungs to stop taking in air and letting it out. It twisted in him as he thought of those monks, some not much older than himself, who lived at the abbey and took instruction in Latin and lettering, who could put the work of their hands on sheets of parchment, or vellum. Men whose life's labor was to write books—to illuminate pages, in real paint.

Oh, he would be willing to work and study all his life, to leave his mother and Kerry, to live until death in silent austerity if once before that he could illumine, on vellum, one page of his own.

A single page, and his life would have counted for something.

In back of him, not two miles from where he stood in this aching, jealous, altogether sinful state, were the monks of the abbey, cherished like sheep—not for milk and wool, but for their prayers and their learning. Ahead was his crowded, noisy home, and his father in a fume, a switch handy.

Ahead was his empty, unlettered life, and no escape.

In the wattle-fenced yard that surrounded his father's house he turned again to gaze at the abbey buildings on their distant cliff. Were they all sons of the gentry and nobility up there? He did not see how that could be.

Surely *anyone* could have a call to serve Heaven in the cloistered life. If called—could even a farmer's son be refused entry?

There was error in this reasoning, and Cormac,

though he lied for art's sake, could not lie to God. He did not feel called to serve Heaven. His was a call to learn letters and Latin. And Irish and Greek.

He wanted to make books. To write sagas of Irish history, and poems. To copy the gospels. And then— oh, should it please God—to draw, in jeweled paints, splendid and intricate pictures to His glory.

These were foolish, stubborn dreams. And hopeless.

Feet dragging, he walked over the croft to his doorstep. His father's dog, Mag, lay in the yard, head on her paws. She would not come into the house at any time, even in rough weather choosing the barn.

Who can blame her? Cormac thought, stooping to put Pangur Ban next to the dog's shaggy shoulder. There's little peace or joy under this rooftree.

He put his own shoulders back and walked into the house, leaving Pangur Ban nestled close to Mag.

And he envied them, too.

Envied their simple unenvious lives.

CHAPTER II

N THE DOORSILL he stood a moment, eyes on his father's back. Liam Brudair's temper was constant, like a damped-down turf fire, but now it was flaring.

"Where is he, wife? I'll have an answer this instant."

Cormac wondered that his mother could look up calmly from the corner where she was carding wool, drawing the metal-toothed comb through long tangled strands.

"Cormac, you mean?" she asked.

"Who else would I be meaning but Cormac? He is not in the upper pasture, repairing the wall, where I left him this forenoon after the apple picking, and nor is he in the garden gathering vegetables with the others, and so where has he got to, answer me."

The boy in the doorway hunched and tightened his jaw. Oh, his da was furious this time, no question.

Yet Megeen Brudair shrugged as if nothing was amiss. "I let him go," she said. "For a little while is all. He worked hard at the apple picking all morning and I thought it no harm to—"

Brudair made an impatient gesture. "The day that one works hard I'll petition the abbot to have him canonized. Gathering apples is not work, it's child's play. And the mending of the wall would require an hour, no more. I ask you again, wife. *Where is he?*"

"Sure, I haven't a notion, Liam. About. About somewhere. Why not call him?"

"I have been calling him—"

Drawing a deep breath, Cormac stepped into the bare room. "Here I am, Da."

His father spun about. A tall man, in homespun smock, working trousers wrapped to the knees like a cottier's. He had two shirts, two pair of leather boots—one rough, one fine—and a cloak with a metal brooch to fasten it by. But Liam Brudair cared little for how he looked. "As I work like a slave in the Wicklow tin mines," he would say, "what use to dress as if I did not?"

Now he fixed hard eyes on this, his eldest son. "I ask you—calmly now—where have you been the past hour?"

Cormac swallowed, turned his head from side to side, remained silent, lips tight.

A moment passed, then Liam took the birch switch

12

from a nail on the wall where it hung and said, "Come."

"Liam—" Megeen began. She broke off at her husband's glance.

"It's all right, Mither," Cormac whispered, following his father out of the cottage, across the croft where the very geese scattered as if aware of trouble, and into the barn.

Brudair pointed to a wooden tub. "Bend."

Cormac leaned, head on his arms, and prepared himself.

"I will give you a further chance," said his father, "to confess your whereabouts, to beg my pardon for your boneheaded idle ways, your shirking and shrinking—" He waited, then roared, "Before God, I can make nothing of you—fourteen years old and a body would think you'd lost the use of your arms like an old man. Your brothers work circles around you! The baby Brendan himself contributes more than you do— at least he answers when spoken to! Will you or will you not tell me where you have been, where you go when you sneak off from the labor the rest of us do willingly—"

"I do my share!" Cormac said boldly, lifting his head.

Down came the switch on his buttocks. The pain seemed to lance up to his throat. Most times his father used the switch lightly, as if not convinced he was right, this instance, to use it at all. Today his rage permitted no doubts.

13

Unfair, unfair, Cormac cried to himself, trying not to cry aloud. He isn't fair! I labor with the rest and *sneak off* hardly ever at all, being given little chance.

But he would not, though the pain were ten times this—though how it could be he did not—he gasped—never would he reveal—betray—his dreams to his father....

"Stop!" he screamed. "Da, for God's sake, stop now!"

Holding the birch aloft, Brudair said, "The answer to me question—quick now!"

"I just—walk," Cormac said, straightening with a tentative air. Shivering with pain, he knew he might have to go back over the tub, but found relief in standing upright for a moment.

"Walk, is it! *Walk!* Walk where, walk why . . . what do you mean, *walk?*"

"To have time to meself, and that's all about it. I don't do anything wrong—" Lie! Or—not a lie? Was it so wrong—was it wrong at all—to want to escape the mulelike existence that lay ahead of him on the farm, to want to learn, to long to read letters, to write—to *paint?*

"Da," he pleaded, "don't *you* ever get sick of—" he began, but met his father's eyes, and faltered.

"Sick of what?" Liam Brudair said in a dangerous voice.

Cormac licked his lips, ran a hand across his mouth. "Of working like a slave in the Wicklow mines," he said in a burst of inspiration. He watched his father, seeking a reaction.

14

"Ah, devil take me," said the farmer, tossing the switch on the floor. "Pick that thing up," he directed, and turned away, shoulders bent. For a second, as he left the barn, he seemed to stumble.

Cormac, in a rush of what he could not believe was pity—pity Liam Brudair?—ran in pursuit.

"Da," he said, pulling at the big man's sleeve. "Da, I'm sorry I vex you. I'll—I'll work harder, see if I don't—"

Brudair glanced down, made as if to speak, then strode on unspeaking, leaving Cormac to follow with the switch, which he put carefully back on the nail, as they all did after a chastisement.

Cormac started to sit, changed his mind. He thought he was probably bleeding through his hose, but would not look.

I'm the one, he thought, who gets to hang up the switch most times. His younger brothers—Kerry, Natt, and Dal—did little to earn their father's displeasure, and Brudair would not lift a hand to Meg, six years old. What gentleness he had was for women—his wife, his old mother who lived in the cottage with them, and the girl Meg. Brendan, the baby, he still treated with absentminded fondness. Cormac wondered if he'd been so to his other sons when they were infants at nurse.

Does he grow hard when we seem old enough not to bend under his hand? Old enough to shoulder our share of the striving from sunrise to dark in field and barn, turf bog and sheep pasture, copse and furrow—

the oxlike drudgery that gives us food, and this roof. That keeps off the cold.

Little more it gains us, thought Cormac. Little more. There is never time to stop, think, stare about, and wonder at the strangeness, the beauty and horror of God's world. No chance to be idle, to loll in dreams, in wishes.

There was a saying in the glen—*burning daylight.*

It was burning daylight if his mother lit a rush candle before day had died away outside entirely, even though—within the windowless cottage—they could scarce see one another's faces. It was burning daylight if a person stopped to rest, or even nod for a moment during the long hours between dawn and dusk.

What would they call daydreaming?

His father would call it a conflagration, and soon put it out, though in doing so he drowned the dreamer, and left him lifeless.

This day, with the storm grumbling over the ocean but remaining offshore, they would cart the apple tribute to the Ui Niall's castle, and so would have their midday meal here in the cottage.

When guarding sheep on the far hillside, the boys took food for themselves and for Mag, since they remained at night, lying under heaven in good weather, sheltering within the stone byre in bad. Cormac, with Kerry, was set to keep watch for a week. Then Dal would go out with Natt. So they alternated the summer long, until the time, just past, when they drove the flock down to winter within the walls of their holding.

16

When in the fields—plowing, sowing, reaping according to the season—when cutting blocks in the peat bogs, or when with neighboring children they scoured the forest—by permission of the Ui Niall—seeking fallen branches, coppice, for fuel, or beechnut mast for their boar, then Meg fetched food out to them in a basket. Oatcakes, a turnip or bit of fruit, a jug of cider.

It was then they could rest for half an hour, too tired usually even to speak. From Cormac's view, it was as well. He did not accord well with his brothers, except for Kerry, who was dear to him as a—well, he would not say "brother" since his other brothers were not dear to him. Kerry was his friend, his companion, the only person in all his world that he could laugh with.

Dal, at eleven, three years younger than Cormac, was as hardworking as Brudair himself, and held Cormac in contempt for reasons he thought his own but were reflections of their father's. Natt, slave to Dal, scarcely eight years old, shared Dal's attitudes in all matters. He never reasoned.

"We'll take our food to the barn and eat as we put the root vegetables down in sand," Brudair said now, standing. He never sat in the house, and only lay down to sleep. "Come, boys."

"No," said his wife. "Let them stay and rest a bit." She smiled at her husband. "Keep me company a bit, as you do not."

Liam shook his head at her folly, rested a hand briefly on the shawled shoulder of his old and silent

17

mother, then strode from the cottage, followed by Dal and Natt.

As they went out, Pangur Ban entered, crossed the floor to where Cormac had lowered himself cautiously to a straw pallet, and climbed on his lap, purring, butting his head against Cormac's face.

"Well," said Megeen, picking Brendan up and dandling him. "Here we are—the idle ones." She smiled mischievously at Kerry and Cormac. "Quick, how shall we make the most of it?"

"Tell us about the Northmen," said Kerry. "Tell us how they blazed across the sea in their longboats, and you fled with your sisters to the forest—I like to hear of it, now they don't come anymore." It was said that the Vikings had turned their terrible attention to lands beyond Britain itself.

Megeen Brudair crossed herself. "Holy Mary, keep them from us," she prayed, yet in a moment began to tell of the time, when she was but a child, that the last invasion of the Northmen, said to be Danes, took place on this west coast of Ireland.

The women of the glen were the tale-spinners, the tellers of Irish history, of olden times before Saint Patrick, when the people worshiped rivers and trees, badgers and wolves and curious stones. Times when Cuchulainn and his warriors of the Red Branch, savage and valorous, swung their three-ridged battle swords and caused lesser chiefs to tremble the length of all Ireland.

The Irish chiefs of later days, however proud and rocklike in bravery, had never prevailed against marauding Northmen. Megeen told her sons how these chiefs, calling themselves "kings," held princely courts all over the country, in imitation of King Alfred of Britain.

"And the fact of it is," she would say, "their ancestors were High Chiefs who a long—oh a long ago—gained the power over their neighbors. Through strength, or cunning, or treachery. It's all one to them. Had chance fallen differently, generations back, Himself, your own da, might be 'the Brudair,' and he receiving tribute from Con Ui Niall, yeoman. It is just how things fell out, a long ago."

It was said that the da of the da of the da of the da of this Ui Niall, when asked by what right he held his land, replied, "By the right of my sword—how shall I say else?" His descendants had been saying it ever since, increasing their lands by the right of their swords.

The border battles of Irish chiefs, conducted by daylight, called off at dark, resumed next morning if both parties agreed, caused havoc, often destruction of lands and livestock held by their tenants, for whom they had use but no respect. There was little bloodshed. Their battles, said Megeen, were as children's games compared to an invasion by the Viking tribes, the scourge of the earth.

"They came in fleets," she said now, in the singsong lilt of the tale-spinner, "in dragon-prowed longboats

19

twenty oars to a side. Their sails were woolen, striped in wild colors. Bronze shields lined the gunwales. They were tall as stone towers, muscled and fanged like beasts, and they jangling with the gold—bracelets and necklaces and anklets and armlets. They had the yellow hair and beards on them, streaming in dirty tangles. Oh, they laid everything waste. All, all was ground under their stone heels, no quarter given. Oh, nothing, no one could draw their pity—not children or women, not priests or monks . . . nor could our battle-tempered, wild-tempered Irish warriors stand against them, for all that their challenges rang to burst the air apart. . . ."

She bowed her head, lifted it, sang on. "They knew not God, these beasts in man's forms. I was but a child when last they came—God keep them ever from us—and my da gathered us together, the way we escaped into the forest and many neighbors with us but some stayed, to their sorrow. Oh, ah—we lived in cairns and bear caves, on roots and berries and returned weeks later to find neighbors and cattle slaughtered, fields and farms burned, the very abbey ransacked, monks murdered, the castle raided and left in ruins. . . ."

She told how the Ui Niall of that day was taken away in chains with most of his men, and heard of no more. But his eldest son had escaped and rebuilt, and resumed his fief, with no complaints from the men of the glen. Why? Cormac wondered. "Why did the yeomen not fight him?" he asked.

"Fight him?" said Megeen.

"Why did they not contest his right to be *the* Ui Niall?"

"How contest it?" asked his mother in bewilderment. "It was his right."

Even Kerry looked confounded and Cormac shrugged and subsided.

Megeen, saddened, tired, gestured toward her husband's mother. "She's the one could tell you the tales. A grand spinner she was in her day, and not just of cloth." She closed her eyes briefly. "Look at what we come to, boys, do we live long enough."

At the center hearth with the smokehole above it crouched Gammer, Liam Brudair's mother. Shawled, though the autumn day was warm. Silent, though once she had been a great talker, a grand spinner of tales. Stooped, though she had been, said their own mother, straight and fine-looking. She stirred the pot of boiled kale and beans with trembling hands.

She was able still to tend the turf fire, make the broth, the stirabout. Twice weekly she swept rushes from the hard earth floor and strewed it afresh. Until recently she had milked their cow, Jemmy, and done the churning, knowing to the second when the cream separated from the milk. This chore was now Cormac's, the only one he did willingly.

The old woman earned her keep still. No man, or woman, Brudair said, could call life wasted while still able to work.

Cormac, looking at his aged grandmother, asked

himself if a life that had been labor and nothing else could not be called wasted altogether. Was such a life worth having? He shuddered at the blasphemy. All lives were precious, even the meanest. Abbot Maher and Prior Aelric of the abbey said so, and they could not be mistaken.

Yet all around him in the glen it seemed that people lived like the very farm creatures. Working, eating, sleeping like Bos, their ox. He never lifted his head, was unaware of other lives than his own, heedless of suffering not his own. Bos didn't think about himself, he just did what he was driven to do. Like Himself, thought Cormac, like me da.

But was this a life for a *man* to live? Or—he looked at his mother, grown quiet, nursing Brendan—was this all his mother would ever know—bearing the children of an unsmiling man, wearing out her days and her beauty for them and him?

Where did these ideas come from? He dared not share them even with Kerry, yet stubbornly continued to feel that a life empty of learning, of curiosity about beings other than yourself, lands other than your own, that an existence that never took into account how the ragged robin was ruffled at its edges, how the lapwing turned somersaults as it flew, that a whole life spent without seeing that there was beauty in the world, or caring that there was misery, *was not a life worth having.*

He stroked his kitten, and thought that somewhere in that small, perfectly shaped, long-whiskered head, behind those eyes that widened to spheres and narrowed to slits, was a mind that comprehended something other than itself. He thought that Pangur Ban, nudging his hand, purring, pawing, knew *him*, Cormac Brudair.

That Pangur Ban loved him, he truly believed.

CHAPTER III

ERRY AND CORMAC
sat in the cart, steady-
ing two enormous leather buckets filled with apples.

"First to the castle, is it not, Cormac?" This was
Kerry's first trip with the tithe, and he was breathtaken
with the excitement of it.

"Always first to the castle, so they can make sure
of getting the pick of the crop."

"There's no difference between the two pickings."

"The castle steward thinks that if he pinches his
chin and looks from one bucket to the other, frowning
and sucking his teeth, and then—" Cormac selected
an apple, turned it round and round, moved it from
one hand to the other, sniffed at the stem and, curling
his lips with an air of suspicion, put his teeth to it—

"then does *that* with a pome from each bucket, he can tell which is worthy of the castle. After he's gone through allsuch fiddle-fa, he points to your bucket, or to mine, it really makes no difference, and says, 'Those for my lord, farmer!' Might's well eat this," he added. "You have one, too."

Kerry grinned, looking forward to the steward's performance.

Bos, the bullock, trudged along the rocky upward path, led by Liam, who would not give him extra weight to carry. Mag walked beside, swinging her tail. When one of the two large wooden wheels dipped into a rut, both boys braced their bodies against the buckets to keep them from tipping. Even so, a few fruits spilled out and rolled to the road. Each time a halt was called to fetch them back.

They passed a field where a tardy neighbor and his sons were gathering windrows of hay to store in their barn, fodder for winter feeding of stock. In those barns, larger than the houses they lived in, no matter how many were in the family, farmers stacked, for winter fires, turf that had been cut in summer on the peat banks. Sorted and spread, too, were apples and onions, peaches, pease, dried plums. Root vegetables were put down in sand, hauled from the shore. Each barn had a flitch of bacon hanging from a beam— hogs too greedy to be wintered over. Every farmer's barn was precisely like his neighbor's, but the Brudairs' was always full betimes, Liam not holding with delay of any sort, in any area of life.

25

He and the boys lifted hailing hands and were greeted in turn.

"To the castle?" yelled Hugh Boyle, a burly man, late always in every area of life.

Liam nodded. "None too soon, either," he said, in a tone of meaning.

Hugh Boyle laughed. "I'll get around to it in me own time," he said. "I've already taken up a cartload of firewood—coppice, mostly, but a few logs, too. And the hams of me boar they've had too. They can wait for the rest, filthy robbers."

Liam nodded again.

Presently the way led along lanes of holly trees, dark-leaved, with bright berries, and fuchsia bushes, now blossomless. In spring and summer the heavy-headed purple and yellow flowers made the countryside ring with color. And in spring white apple blossoms and pink plum blossoms filled the air with sweetness.

"Spring's the best time," Cormac said now.

"I guess," said Kerry. "Anyway, I don't like winter."

They shivered, anticipating cold dawns coming, when they would rise just before sunup, eat their porridge by rushlight, and stump out to begin chores in the chill gray morning, and sometimes through freezing sleet, or deep snow.

"Wicked cold, winter is," said Cormac.

Worse than that, for him. No escape to his badger set in the months from Advent to Lent. If the season was uncommonly severe, to Easter itself. During those long, lightless, icicle-hung weeks, he would create pictures in his head, trying to store the memory of them for spring, not minding what he lost since more would crowd into his mind. This brain of his so jostled with drawings of creatures and plants, birds and fish, that he'd grow dazed, heedless of activity around him, till his father would throw up his hands and shout, "Is it a booby you are, at all, you gormless calf?"

Cormac, jerked out of painted dreams, would leap to his feet and ask what it was had been asked of him, so that he could hasten to do it.

Sometimes he felt sorry for his father.

The brothers were silent for a while, bumping along, the wheels of the cart creaking, the leather buckets budging heavily, as if alive.

Presently Kerry said, "Does the switch hurt you now, Cormac?" He had, himself, done nothing so far to earn any but the mildest switching, but thought it could not be too painful for Cormac, who let out no sound while the chastening took place—in the barn, away from the sight of children "innocent of wrong-doing," their father would grumble, scowling at Cormac.

"I don't mind it," Cormac said. "Da has the light hand mostly, for all he bellows." Today the hand had been heavy enough, and yet—

"You know," he went on, checking to be sure his father was out of hearing, "I don't think he likes to whip me. I think he thinks it's his duty. Da always does his duty."

"Oh, yes," Kerry said. "That he does. And that he should, too. Don't you think?" he added.

"Sure and you're right, Kerry. A man's got to do by his children as he thinks fitting. Only—"

"Only what?" Kerry insisted. He was devoured with curiosity about what it could be that Cormac thought worth getting even light switchings for, again and again. His brother would never tell why he went off in the way he did, sometimes not coming home for hours, claiming, when he did get back, to have been after counting sheep, tracking a stray, or mending a distant withy fence or wall that no one could say had *not* been knocked down by a neighbor's ox.

Kerry didn't think Cormac was rounding up stray lambs or fixing the withes of a fence or replacing the stones of a wall, those times when he disappeared. He was up to something, only what could it be?

"Cormac—" he began, but just then they turned a bend in the road and the great gray castle seemed to spring up before them, invisible one moment, vast and lowering the next. Kerry gasped at its suddenness, at its size. Walled and moated, with two round towers that had arrow slits high up for archers to aim through. There was a great stone archway with a carved shield at its peak, showing a swan tangled with a—a leopard—Kerry thought, peering upward.

He whistled. "Gorra, Cor. Did you ever see the like?"

"Da says it's but a measly barracks, not to compare with the splendid castles in the east."

But Cormac, too, felt overwhelmed.

They rattled over a stone causeway, across the bridge, and drew up at the gatehouse where two brawny soldiers with long mustaches stood, arms crossed, at either side of the entrance to a stone tunnel. They wore helmets and leather cuirasses, but were otherwise unarmored.

"Your business?" one demanded.

"Man," said Liam impatiently, waving toward his cart, "can you not see what my business is? I'm bringing apples in tribute, just as last week I brought logs, and the week before that grain and the week before *that* corn from my mill, and two fine fleeces, and the two of you here each time, asking after my *business*, as if it were any of yours...."

"You've got the tongue on you, Brudair," the soldier said, but waved them on.

Trundling through the dank tunnel, they emerged into the bailey, a vast courtyard, where Liam pulled Bos to a stop and stood, running a hand down the bullock's neck and staring about angrily.

"What's wrong?" Kerry asked against his brother's ear.

"It's always like this when we come to the castle."

"Why?"

Cormac let out a long breath. "Da doesn't like the way they look upon us here, as if we were cottiers, or slaves. We're as good as anybody, he says."

"And are we not, then?"

"Of course we are. But if people think they're better than you are, and yourself in no position to prove them wrong—well, wouldn't it make you angry?"

Kerry considered. "I don't think I'd care what they thought."

29

"Maybe so," said his brother, as a man came striding toward them over the cobbles. "Maybe we'll find out this day if you'd care or not."

"Is this the steward?" Kerry asked.

"A porter. A lackey—being sent ahead to look at us, so. Then to go back and tell the steward that we're here."

"He has nice clothes," said Kerry, eyeing the linen tunic, and the woolen cloak that was dyed blue and fastened with a brooch.

"Wait till you see what his nibs will be wearing."

"Can't the steward see for himself that we're here?"

"Of course he can. He likes to have lackeys announce him. Just as he has to announce the knights who announce the Ui Niall. They set store by such things—lackeys bowing to stewards, stewards bending the knee to knights, knights groveling to chiefs and High Kings."

"Must the Ui Niall grovel to anyone?"

"Eoghan, the High King at Tara, says Mither. She says he'll never do it, though, since the High King doesn't come here and the—what would you call him, the Low King?—anyway, he doesn't go there."

"Such doings," said Kerry, impressed.

The porter approached and looked into the cart.

"Apples, I see."

Liam narrowed his eyes and said nothing, though the man waited for a sign of humility, fixing his gaze on the farmer's cap. Liam stared stubbornly back,

30

making no move to doff it. At his side, Mag curled her lips, baring fine white teeth.

The lackey glanced at her, stepped back, and said peevishly, "I'll announce you."

"Do that," Liam growled, reaching down to pull Mag's ear. "That's not worth the snarl, my girl," he whispered to her. "Your descent is longer than his, and your looks and manners better."

Presently a man in a white linen tunic strode toward them over the cobbles. His cloak of crimson wool, with a narrow embroidered border, was fastened by an elaborate bronze brooch. Low on his waist he wore a leather belt from which hung a sheathed dagger and a large ring of keys.

"I am informed that you are here with the apple tribute," he said, and waited, eyes on Brudair's cap.

Liam's mouth tightened. He hesitated, then slowly lifted his hand and dragged the cap off.

Satisfied, the steward moved to the cart and eyed the leather containers. He looked from one to the other for a long time, pinching the tip of his chin, running his tongue over his teeth, before reaching to select an apple from the bucket Kerry had had in charge. Turning it slowly, he put it to his nose, sniffed the stem, put it aside, and plucked from Cormac's bucket, repeating the performance. Baring his teeth, he took a gingerly bite, chewed, closed his eyes, smacked his lips, put that apple down, took up the first, and sampled it.

Kerry and Cormac, hugging themselves, tried not to

31

laugh, but noticing how their father was shaken with rage, all at once found nothing funny.

The steward snapped his fingers, pointed to Kerry's fruit.

"*This* for the Ui Niall," he snapped, adding, "Not up to standard, this crop, is it, cottier?"

"*Yeoman!*" said Liam. "Liam Brudair, yeoman, free-holder."

"Of course. I keep forgetting." The steward turned away, turned back. "You know where to take them— to the souterrain."

He strutted away, cape swinging.

Liam leaned his head against Bos, straightened after a moment and said, "Get the small buckets, boys."

For an hour they transferred the apples of choice from large to small buckets, and carried what they knew to be as fine a crop as the orchard had ever produced down a winding stone stairway to a cold underground storeroom, the souterrain.

They did not speak again until they'd turned the bend in the road, leaving the castle behind.

"Well," Liam said heavily, "it's done. That's the last of it till spring. A dear price to pay for protection."

"What are they protecting us from, Da?" Kerry asked. "The countryside is quiet. There aren't even border skirmishes going on of late."

"Hah." Liam bit his lip, clucked to Bos. "They protect us from what *might* happen. And doubtless *will* happen, though not for some months now. They hang up their battle-axes and shields when winter sets in, doughty warriors that they are."

"Why do they fight then, at all?"

"God knows," said their father. "Or I suppose He knows, and it isn't for us to question His ways." He thought a moment. "God can't be bending the eye every minute on every stupid Irish chieftain's tribe. We must thank Him for keeping the Vikings from our shores these many years—since it's little enough protection the Ui Nialls and the O'Haras and the Tyrones would be giving us should the Northmen come again. They might stand fast and fight in their own fortresses. I doubt not they would—after all they are Irish and valorous if foolhardy—but for us in the countryside, we'd be looking to ourselves for protection."

"Then why are we—" Kerry began again, and was interrupted.

"The Ui Niall, my boy, keeps the Tyrones and the O'Haras from laying waste our homes, our fields, our lives. Therefore we pay tribute to the castle, and take the insolence of that jumped-up varlet, the steward. And that's all about it."

"Why then do we give to the abbey, Da?" said Kerry. "They can't fight. They don't protect us."

"Never say so," his father answered. "The good monks and the priests, Father Maher and Prior Aelric, pray for us. I put greater store in the protection of their prayers than in all the bowmen the castle could muster."

He turned Bos onto the rocky sledge road leading to the cliff's summit and the monastery, which was low walled, with a gate open to every seeker of peace and sanctuary.

As they climbed, a soft rain, smelling of leaf mold and mushrooms, began to fall.

CHAPTER IV

ARLY DECEMBER, be-
fore daybreak. Carrying a
horn lantern, Cormac stepped out of the house, rub-
bing his eyes. He was bundled against the cold, a
shawl over his homespun smock, leather boots to his
feet.

In the night snow had started falling, and was
coming down still over farm, fields, and pasture—all
lying now under a rumpled white mantle. Branches of
trees were sleeved in fluff, the croft lacy with tracks of
geese that trudged about, dipping their bills, seeking
seeds. When Cormac appeared, they waddled after
him, honking.

"A good morning to you," he said, regarding them
fondly.

Swirling snowflakes flew against his face, into his

eyes, onto his thick dark hair. No matter the cold, it was indeed a good morning, so clean-seeming in its whiteness.

Whistling, he went into the barn, took down a wooden bucket, set it under Jemmy, positioned himself on the milking stool, and leaned his head against her warm flank, smiling when she turned her head to fix him with lake-brown eyes. Her breath mingled with his—hers hay sweet. His own, he supposed, smelled of his breakfast—dried apples and cheese.

Her calf, that had no name, he'd secured to a post. The spindle-legged creature watched the procedure through long-lashed eyes, still a milky blue, and awaited its turn without uproar. Some calves in the like situation kicked and bellowed, claiming to be cheated of their rights.

"Do you trust me, then?" Cormac asked it gently. "Sure, you make no mistake. Your mother and I have you in mind, no fear."

He treasured the time he spent at dawn and at dusk in the barn, milking Jemmy. It amused him, today, to be watched by sweet silly-faced sheep who crowded in their pen, bleating hoarsely in a way Cormac found altogether pleasant. They'd been brought in from the open-sided fold when the weather turned harsh. Pangur Ban, no longer a kitten, had drunk several squirts of milk aimed at his open pink mouth, and sat now on top of an old ewe, washing his face.

"Peaceful, peaceful," Cormac murmured, wishing Jemmy were six cows, to keep him here all morning, and again all evening.

———

During these months when the sun, seeming somehow faded, rose late, and early sagged into the western
horizon, work was light on the land, and farm life easy.
Too easy, with little to do, little relief from one another,
crowded as they were in the two rooms. The boys
slept together in the back, on the one wide pallet—
Pangur Ban nestled against Cormac's shoulder. Meg
and Gammer slept together across the room, while
their parents put down a bed in the front. Jostled this
way, the family grew irritable, finding relief by day in
long walks.

At rare times their mother and father would go of
an evening to visit Hugh Boyle and his wife, to take a
glass with them and exchange views. This did not
occur frequently because Brudair and Boyle always
ended up quarreling. Or, Cormac thought, Da quarrels
and Hugh Boyle laughs, which sets me father fuming,
which makes Boyle laugh the more, so it's not to be
wondered at that they can't be long in each other's
company, but is a pity all the same, they being the
only family in the glen nearby enough to be called
neighbors.

Day followed day, moistly chill, and at times bitter
indeed. Under low gray skies Liam would tramp for
hours with his dog, then come home to sit shivering
near the huskily murmuring peat fire, short of words,
short of temper.

The boys, Dal, Natt, and Kerry, would scamper away
early to run across the stubble of bare, ice-rimed
fields, playing tag, tossing stones at rooks, returning

37

to snatch a bit of bread and cheese, or an oatcake, a turnip, before racing off again, unless hard weather confined them altogether, when they would go into the back room, away from grown-ups, and devise games to pass the long hours.

Cormac thought they spent their time tumbling like fox kits so as to be tired enough to fall asleep right after supper. In order—actually—not to be obliged to sit under the critical eye of their father, who had little to do, now, with his own time, but appeared to feel that somebody should be accomplishing something.

It was then that women were best off, theirs being year-round work. They had cooking and cleaning to do each day, making the broth, the stirabout, baking bread and oakcakes in their stone oven. There was the carding of wool, the spinning, the mending of clothes. The making of new homespun garments to replace those worn past repair. Nothing was discarded. Old clothes were used for rags, for patching, for potholders, for wicks to float in oil in the two horn lamps they owned.

Once a month, on a sunny day, the family wash was done out in the croft. Water fetched from the brook was put in an enormous basin into which they dropped heated stones. Their garments, and the sacks that enclosed their straw pallets, were stirred with harsh soap, then hedge-spread to dry.

Meg, too, now that she was old enough, took her place at the spinning wheel, the stewpot, the washing basin. She employed the besom to sweep old rushes out the front door, replacing Gammer at that task.

Gammer now always sat silent in a corner, her life's labor ended.

The boys strewed fresh rushes on the earth floor, carried in peat blocks for the fire in the center hearth that was not allowed to go out and coppice for the oven. Daily they went to the springhouse to fetch jugs of cider, and of milk. They fetched in small wooden tubs of cheese and butter—their own churnings. They were sent the rounds of snares Liam laid for hares, which made good eating. Liam dressed and cooked them outdoors on a spit.

For Dal and Natt, of course, everything done under the thatch was woman's work. Dal said he'd have no part of it, and Natt, who took chores sifted down from his husky older brother, agreed. They willingly helped their father kill hares, or geese, or little bull calves. They assisted in the slaughter of livestock not to be wintered over.

Cormac and Kerry, contemptuously excused from these duties, and desperate for occupation, offered to help with household chores. But to that Brudair would lift a forbidding hand. "You'll none of you be doing woman's work. Even"—fixing his eye on Cormac—"even if you be fit for it."

"I get that tired of playing games," Kerry said to Cormac, "I'd like to take a turn at making the stirabout, or pounding the clothes. Even carding wool for Mither. That looks like fun—making the tangles come out, smoothing it into long strings."

Cormac agreed entirely, but they knew better than to argue, at any time, with Himself—most especially

39

in winter, when he prowled about, finding everywhere reasons to carp and criticize and complain.

He is not, Cormac realized, absolutely angry with us. It's the way he can't abide not working, so is driven to needless tasks—like repairing thatch not in want of repair—their house snug, top and sides, no chinks for a winter wind to slide through, or rain to ooze through, as at Hugh Boyle's house, where the fire smoked till people choked, and things were always damp.

Brudair fed what stock was left—Jemmy and her calf, a few sheep, a much reduced flock of geese. The hog was gone. He'd devoured all the acorns and beechnuts gathered for him, and there was scant waste from the table to winter him over. He was now two flitches of bacon hanging from a beam in the barn, the rest of him having gone to the castle.

At times, perhaps like his children wanting just to be out of the house, Liam would go to the barn and sort and re-sort apples, putting aside those that were bruised. His mother made a wonderful pudding from windfalls or bruised pomes. Then Liam would whistle to Mag and set off across the fields, as if driven.

In every way, winter was the roughest season.

Now, having got the bucket full enough for the day's supply, Cormac unroped Jemmy's calf. He tottered to his mother and began to shove and buck at the udder, patient no longer.

"Don't be in a panic, so," Cormac said, patting the little rump. "You'll have your share."

He watched the nursing calf sadly. A male it was,

and would go the way of the hog in a month or two. They could not afford his keep. There was but one bull to the twelve yeoman farmers whose holdings were under the Ui Niall, that bull kept by the richest among them.

And this so sweet-tempered, thought Cormac, frowning and shaking his head. His concern for animals was deep—not alone for what was under their care on the farm, but for those creatures that shied from man and his arrows, his snares, his expertly flung stones. He would lie at night, hearing the faraway cry of wolves, the hunting call of owls, the scream of a bobcat, and hope that God had such as these under His eye, as He had the sparrow.

When, occupied at his badger set, he saw a roe deer step delicately through the branchy woods, heard the hedgehog clatter in the brush, now and then spied a vixen with her brood, he would pray for them—that if they were killed it would be without pain, and that when they were dead, their souls would be welcome in Heaven.

He had never asked Father Maher about the souls of animals, for fear of the answer. His own father said they had none, but Cormac did not think his father knew everything.

In hard winters, farm animals were slaughtered that might otherwise have lived longer. And on a stinted holding such as theirs—above the cottiers but way below, say, that of Boyle—a little bull calf stood no more chance than the boar had. Cormac had liked that old hog, with his whiskery snout, his great appetite, his clever little eyes. He liked the geese, who followed people about like members of the family, and produced downy goslings, yellow as gorse, and fine large eggs.

Still—he ate his share of bacon with relish, and even now his mouth watered at the thought of the spit-roasted goose that was an every-year Christmas feast.

On a farm, life was hard, and often sad, but perhaps it was not otherwise in the rest of the world—except for those born to wealth and long-rooted names.

Or—for a monk in an abbey.

His father said that the brothers on the hill labored from sunup to sundown and then had their sleep interrupted the night long for vigil and prayer.

"One way and another," said his da, "I doubt not they get less rest at all than we do."

Oh, how happy would I be, thought Cormac, to sacrifice sleep for the chance to be a Latin-learned monk, working up there in the scriptorium, copying old manuscripts, and perhaps—was it possible—even composing prayers, tales, histories, out of his own head, his own thoughts?

One day, when he went to confess his lies to Father Maher, he would ask the question that had troubled his mind and stirred his heart for more years now than he could readily count.

One day, after Father Maher had said in his dry-humored quiet voice, "Well then, Cormac—the usual penance, increased by two prayers and an additional ten minutes on your knees—," one day he would say,

"Father Maher, I wish to leave the world and enter here to serve God and take instruction in Latin and learning and lettering."

He had not so appealed to the abbot yet, and did not know that ever he would dare, because—as clear in his mind as if spoken aloud in that same dry-humored, quiet voice—he could hear Father Maher's response.

"You wish to enter here, Cormac, to learn. But to serve God? I fear not."

Once that was said, both entreaty and answer would be behind him. This way the dream floated before him, glimmering—like swamp fire—a vision not out of reach, so long as he did not reach for it.

"Come along, now, Pangur," he said to his cat, and started for the springhouse with his bucket. Pangur Ban leaped lightly from the ewe's back and followed him, as he followed always where Cormac led.

"And there's that, too," Cormac said to himself. "Would they let me keep Pangur at all, should I one day be received on the mountain?"

In no way he could picture his life separate from Pangur Ban's.

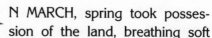

CHAPTER V

N MARCH, spring took possession of the land, breathing soft
airs, sweet airs, teasing pussywillows from their silken
sheaths, coaxing red swamp cabbages to poke their
beaks through fragile layers of ice. At the brook's
edge, almond willows put out yellow fronds, irises
grew in frilly ease, and the striped trout lily came
forth. In the woods, speedwell and bluebells appeared
in the morning that had not been there the night before.

The fluting of the mistle thrush was heard from the
woods, and the drumming of the pied woodpecker. In
fields, over marshes and peat bogs, redwings and
wagtails warbled and chirruped. Now hedge crickets
chirped, and lark and lapwing flew into the clouds and
tumbled out, singing. And now in the barn, on high

beams, chirruping swallows lined their nests of mud and hay with feathers.

Cormac rejoiced to see the return of swallows that came every year to live here and lay their mottled eggs and—he defending them from those ruthless marauders of nests, Dal and Natt—raise their young. He loved to watch them dart from sunlight to raftery shadows, bringing insects to their insatiable nestlings, then to see the nestlings fledge, and, in a short time, fly.

Pangur Ban, watching the progress of the swallows with interest and admiration, now and then caught an inexperienced bird and made off with it, if Cormac was not by to effect a rescue. He did not scold his cat, doing what nature urged upon him.

I suppose, he thought, the grasshopper or the dragonfly, snapped up by the swallow, feels as bad as the fledgling does in Pangur's jaws.

Oh, surely life was a puzzle and seemed to consist of creatures, from man to mole, preying on others in order to live.

"Don't you ever *mind* what it is you do?" he said to Dal, who came striding over the croft, a brace of rabbits dangling from one hand.

Lent and Easter were past, and meat could be eaten again, but Cormac, looking at the little furry bodies matted with blood, the once upright ears hanging so limp, thought maybe the monks were in the right of it, to live on bread and vegetables, a bit of cheese, an egg. Perhaps a fish now and then.

45

"Mind? Whatever do I do that I should be minding it, so?"

"You're forever killing something. You're always *killing*, Dal."

"If I didn't kill them, these'd jump about while we tried to eat them, and there'd be a fuss for you," the younger boy said scornfully. "And I don't suppose you'll turn down your share when they're roasted, cowardly Cor."

"I'm not going to eat meat again at all, and I am not cowardly. I could pin you this moment."

Dal dropped the rabbits, spat on his hands, and crouched.

"Come on," he said. "Try it, me fine brother."

"Ah—what do you suppose? You're three years younger than me—"

"Come on, come on—you're after making the usual feeble excuse because you daren't take me on." Dal darted forward, sprang back in a wide stance, hands spread before him. "Have at you, varlet!"

Cormac shrugged, leaped, feinted, dodged behind Dal, and in a few seconds had his neck in an armlock. So they remained, Cormac keeping his hold—not hard enough to hurt, he hoped—Dal with muscles taut, uttering no sound.

"Here, here!" said Liam Brudair, coming out of the house. "What's this—what are the two of you at now?"

Cormac released his brother and they turned to their father, who shook his head at them and said irritably, "Come now, Cormac, is this the way to be doing, and the boy half your age?"

46

"I'm a lot more than half his age!" Dal protested. "Another couple of years, I'll be twice his size. Then, begob, let him be looking out for himself—"

"The day I have to look out for you, I'll cover meself with ashes and go to keening," Cormac snapped.

"Do you know what, Da?" Dal said, laughing. "The lackwit says he'll not be eating meat again. What do you say to that now?"

"Agh, leave off, leave off, the two of you." Liam glanced at the rabbits, and patted Dal's head. "Good, good. Take them in to your mother. I doubt not when they're served in a stew, Cormac won't be backward at the pot. You both come along and help me yoke Bos to the plow."

Dal brightened. Plowing with his father was as much a delight to him as snaring rabbits and hares, or bringing down rooks with a stone, though he could not yet handle the heavy wooden plow. No one but Himself could do that. So far.

Dal's job was to walk backward, gently waving a peeled hazel wand, coaxing Bos along the furrow with honey words, with promises of the freshest hay, the most loving washing down and brushing and massaging, the sweetest of long lollings in the meadow when plowing should be done.

He found it a pure pleasure and did it better, his father said, nor any other lad in the glen.

Cormac, whose role of ox coaxer had been taken over by Dal, admitted he had never been half so good at it, and it grieved him. Surely he loved animals more than did Dal, so why would the bullock plod after

Dal's voice as though enslaved, pulling the plow through winter-hardened earth, straining those great muscles in mute obedience to a lad's singsong promises?

Like many another question that he posed himself, he had no answer ready. Things were as they were, and that no answer at all, but the best he could do.

His task now was to follow along behind his father, Bos, and Dal, making piles of stones cast up by the plow, which he would then trundle across the field to deposit by the wall.

Hard work it was, that made his back ache and his mind rebel.

"I will never," he said to himself, half attending his Brudair's grunts as he wrestled with the plow, and Dal's minstrelsy to the bullock, "never will I be a farmer.

"I'll go for a soldier first," he said to himself and then snorted.

A soldier, armed with sword or battle-axe or arrow, had the one purpose—to kill living things, animal or human. Not, like Pangur Ban, driven by nature, unaware of the suffering he caused, but able to look his victim in the eye and still drive the sword in.

Never could he be a soldier. I'll be a farmer first, he said to himself and could not keep from laughing.

But—if neither, what then?

A minstrel, maybe? A bard, traveling from castle to castle over the land, even over the seas, singing of battles long past, chanting of deaths cleansed by time of blood and pain and horror.

How merciful was time—that gave a poet leave to

chant of brave men and beautiful ladies, and they clothed in ribbons and veils of heroism. Make-believe. Unbloodied entirely.

To be a bard, welcome in the courts of kings, honored with the "poet's right," he would have to know the epic tales, which he did, having got them from his mother, who chanted them of an evening, she having taken over when Gammer lost the words.

At court, the poets were men. Here in the glen most singers were women, passing the tales down, mother to daughter. But women were not learned, for all their grand memorizing. Their way was not enough for Cormac.

Besides, how sit in castle halls, casting spells with his songs, he who could not tempt an ox down a furrow?

What he wanted, what he had to have if his life was to mean anything, was *learning*. Letters and Latin, that was what he always came back to. So would he not have somehow to persuade Abbot Maher to let him take instruction at the monastery with the promise of one day making his vows?

No answers, no answers . . . to anything he asked himself.

Still he stood motionless, thinking of castles and feasting, of harping, of courtiers richly gowned, and he singing the Irish lays—of Cuchulainn and Conchobar and Fergus of the Brazen Cars. Of lovely women— Deirdre of the Sorrows, Maeve, Cathleen ni Houlihan.

He could not enrapture a bullock, but might he not

capture, enrapture, the grand men and women of Ireland with his voice, his stories? Oh, but no! To sing for the entertainment of High Chiefs like the Úi Niall, for men like that sneering steward, for courtiers who rode over yeomen's pasturelands and tillage lands in pursuit of stags and foxes, not caring what destruction the hunt left behind them?

Never, never sing for such as those.

Never sing at all.

But—to be a monk, living in silence, but able to put his hand to parchment pages—

"Cormac!"

He looked up to find that Dal and his father were a long way off, clear to the end of the field, about to turn back, and here was he, not half down the first row.

Leaning over, picking up earth-caked stones in broken-nailed fingers, he said to himself, "I cannot be a bard, I could never be a soldier, I will not be a farmer. . . ."

Therefore, somehow, he must find his way into the sanctuary of the abbey.

He looked upward. Clouds moved lazily along, whiter than sheep's fleeces, which were not white at all but a sort of yellow—not that the sheep could help that and there were, besides, three black ones in the flock, darker than rain clouds.

Where did black sheep come from?

He gazed beyond the clouds to the blue sky where Heaven was, surely.

Why did he not feel the call to God? He had prayed for a call, waited and prayed. It did not come. Always he knew that what he wanted was not to serve his Heavenly Father, but to satisfy this earthly longing to know letters, to draw, to paint pictures.

Absorbed in thought, perplexed, anxious, he stood with a stone in his hand, looking upward and inward. Until now, he had asked God please to give him a signal, let him have an unmistakable sign that he could take to Abbot Maher and say, "Look, Father Abbot—here's this token I have had from Heaven, and now surely you must let me in."

There was this difficulty—that he could not decide how an unmistakable sign would present itself. All well to say, in his own head, "Look, Father Abbot—" But what would he offer the abbot to look at?

How did God give His signs?

Have I, he wondered, been going at this the wrong way? Instead of asking for a token that maybe God didn't even know he was expecting, should he present a case, put his predicament up to Heaven in a sensible downright manner, leaving no loopholes?

He began to form what seemed to him a reasonable petition, worthy of his Creator's attention. "Isn't it wanting to serve You, in my way, if I want to write out the scriptures in a beautiful hand and paint pictures to Your glory? I mean, if You'll just look at it from my point of view..."

He let the stone fall.

What he wanted, and not God or Father Maher or Prior Aelric would be conned, was to write poetry, pen

51

epics of Ireland and her saints, tales of her stirring
past, descriptions of her green meadows, her tree-
lined lanes and boreens, her hills, the wild sea bridling
on rocky shores, the wild birds nesting on the cliffs.
He longed to paint pictures of her birds and shy
beasts and flowering hedges—

He would, if he had letters, write a history of Ireland
herself, or of her saints...

"Cormac! What are you blethering there for, talking to yourself like a lackwit? What *is* it about you,
you—"

Gormless calf, Cormac said silently.

"—gormless calf!" Liam Brudair said in a tone of
fury.

Here were Dal, Bos, and his father, halted beside
him in the next furrow over.

Since no explanation would serve, Cormac bent to
pick up stones. Dal, with a shrug, resumed his backward march, waving his hazel whip, crooning to the
heavy-shouldered bullock, who trudged, entranced,
dragging the great plow that was gripped in the hands
of a sweating and angry Liam Brudair.

CHAPTER VI

"ERRY," Cormac whispered, "come with me—but be quiet. I don't want the others to hear."

It was a summer morning, their father absent from the farm on sheep business.

"Don't want us to hear what?" asked Dal, appearing silently in the way he had. It's what makes him such a grand success as a hunter, Cormac thought with exasperation.

"I don't want you to hear what I want to say to Kerry, and how can I put it plainer?"

"You can't. Only I want to hear, whatever it is, and I'm going to, but it's probably nothing at all."

"Then why do you—" Cormac began, and left off. There was no handling Dal when he had a mindset, and Dal did not propose to be left out of whispers. Whispers meant secrets and any secret going, Dal was going to be in on, if only to sneer at.

"Me too," said Natt, coming around the side of the house. "Let me too hear. What are you and Cor up to, Kerry?"

"I don't know," Kerry said.

"Oh, sure you don't know."

"It's truth. Cormac didn't get 'round to telling me yet."

"And I'm not going to," Cormac said angrily, knowing that if he did not, this rare chance would be lost. How did he know when the otters would return to the millrace and play their marvelous game that so far only he knew about?

But if he let Dal and Natt—who could be twins in their thinking—if he let them in on this, who knew what they'd do? Laugh? Make a lot of racket and scare the otters away?

Throw stones at them?

He stood, lips tight with indecision. Minutes passed while Kerry looked at him with commiseration, and Dal with revolting confidence. How is it he knows, Cormac wondered, when it's all one to me whether I tell or not, and when, as now, it matters to me so much that I'll be obliged to let him in on it?

Gammer, it was said, had been a "seer," before she and her wits parted company. She had been gifted to look into the future, into people's minds, to spy out their wishes, tell if their hopes would be realized, predict when they would die.

She had been, their mother said, nearly tried for a witch when she was young.

"A witch?" they'd exclaimed, astonished at the thought of Gammer young, of anything she said or did being heeded.

"It was held that she put a spell on anyone she took against. They claimed she caused cows to dry up, and changed folks into bats—spiteful nonsense, you can see." She'd paused, looking inward, and added in a troubled voice, "She said that one day—" Another pause, so long that the children thought she might not continue. She did. "She said one day the Vikings would return to Ireland's shores—God grant she was wrong."

"But if she could cast a spell, so," said Dal, superior to tales of Viking prowess—Irish warriors could crush the fiercest foe on a morning and hold High Court that night—but eager to have someone in the family who could bring misery upon folk she didn't like, "why do you say she was not a witch?"

"Off with you, now. There are no witches, and that's all about it."

Maybe, thought Cormac. Maybe there are not, but should there be, then whatever a male witch is called, Dal is one—the way he knows what I'm thinking, the way he can bring misery on me. Of course, that could come just of his talebearing. Who was it let Da know every time Cormac took off from an assigned duty? Who was it told that he'd not been out on the hill with the sheep, but had left Mag to tend them—Mag doing the better job anyway—while he "sneaked" away?

"Sneaked" was how Dal put it, and—"up to mischief," Dal and Da would conclude between them.

But with all his witchy ways, his brother had never been able to find out where he went or what he did, during those times. Often enough, Dal had tried to follow him, but Cormac was a match for that sort of game. His badger set, holding all that was most important to him—*sacred* to him—that was his secret still. Not even Kerry knew of it.

"Well," Dal said impatiently, "are you going to tell what you and Kerry are plotting, or are you not?"

Still Cormac hesitated, biting his lip.

"All right," he said at length. "But you listen well, Dal. If ever you in the least *way* let on about it, to anybody at all, I will give you a thrashing you'll not forget the rest of your life."

Dal stepped back with a light laugh. "You daren't."

"I dare. I'll do it."

"Da would—"

"I wouldn't mind *what* Da would—so understand that well. If you do anything to spoil—" He stopped, let out a jerky breath. "If you do anything to ruin what I—what we're going to see—I will beat you till you can't stand up, and I won't be after caring in the least what happens to me for the doing of it."

Kerry stared as if Cormac had changed to a wolf in front of his eyes ... this, the mildest, most forgiving, most loving of brothers.

For all Cormac laughed at Dal sometimes, and Natt, too, and other times fell into a rage at their rough and bloody ways, Kerry knew that Cormac felt the blood tie as strongly as anyone else. Families in the glen clung close in these harsh times of border wars, arrogant overlords, uncertain crops, tithes that often left the farm families hungry. Each member defended the others, and Cormac would fight till he dropped, not just for Mither or Gammer or the little ones, but for Dal, Natt, for their da. As Himself would protect Cormac—that he was always baiting and berating—with life itself.

Cormac was strong. He was generous. He refused his share of food when it was scarce, so that Gammer or the baby could eat. He'd help his mother with the heavy work under the thatch, no matter that Dal scoffed.

Cormac was the best brother in the glen. In the world. And never in Kerry's recollection had he heard such threats from that usually patient tongue.

"Cor," he said nervously. "Maybe we better not—whatever it is, let's not do it. I don't think I like this secret."

But Dal put out his hand, saying solemnly, "My word on it, Cor. I will never say anything of what we are about to do, or see, to any soul. Now—*what is it?*"

Cormac wheeled. "Follow me. Quietly, now."

"Where are you going, everybody?" a plaintive voice called from the doorway. They turned back to see Meg, six years old, thumb in mouth, shabby homespun smock hanging any whichway, staring at them with blue beseeching eyes. "Can I come, too?"

"Of course you can't, " Dal snapped. "Girls don't—what makes you think—"

"Please, Cormac," she said, taking a step toward him, her hands clasped, prayerlike. "Let me come see the secret, too?"

Cormac walked back, pulled his sister down on the sill beside him. "He's right, you know, Meg. You can't come with us. Girls can't do things that boys can."

"Why not?"

"Why not?" Cormac looked at her in perplexity. "Because they cannot. You must know that, sister. When are you ever allowed to come with us? You belong in the house with Mither and Gammer. It's your *place*."

Meg wiped a hand across her runny nose. "I don't see why," she said, choking. "Why do I have to have a place and—and boys do not have a place and I not get to do anything ever, or go ever with anybody anywhere—Cormac! It isn't *fair!*"

He stood. "Maybe it is not. I think it is not. But that's how things are, so don't keep asking the why of it. Lasses can't—aren't allowed—wouldn't be able—Oh, stop sniveling!" he said, annoyed and puzzled. "Stay here."

He walked off, refusing to heed his sister's soft sobbing. But when Dal, tapping his forehead with a forefinger, snickered and said, "What a dafty!" Cormac wheeled and said, "You hold your tongue, see? I'd a sight rather have her than you along anywhere, any day." He stumped on, grumbling, leading his brothers over the croft, out the gate, along the cowlane, and down the boreen toward the mill, and he felt that the joy had gone out of this day entirely.

Sorry he was now that he'd thought to invite even Kerry to witness the rapturous game of the otters.

Why couldn't Meg, poor little lass, once in a while do something that was fun? Had Gammer or Mither herself, ever known something, done anything, that was just *fun*, staying in their "place" as they had to? Why did they have to? Why did they stay there, so? If I were a woman, he thought, wouldn't I tell some fool of a man thought he was lord of the world that he was not so, and I'd think for meself and *do* for meself—

No. Not so. If he were a woman—unthinkable to be so—he'd do what women did...he'd keep his place.

Stupid, crazy world.

"I hope the otters aren't there at all," he muttered. "Let them not be there, and I'll never speak of them at all again, not even to Kerry."

Which did not seem fair, surely. Kerry would love the sight of the otters as he did himself.

Dal. Always Dal, putting a blight on things. Nosy, brutish, tattling pest of a Dal, he said to himself, but recalled a time when this brother had been a lad trotting beside him like a new lamb, frisking, turning his head to look up and laugh and say, "Isn't this fun, Cor? Aren't we having fun together?"

It was a recollection painfully fond. How could that small boy, so full of leaping, lamblike spirits, have become the Dal they knew now? Why was it he could

59

never entirely put that other Dal from his mind and so make a thoroughgoing job of disliking this one?

Because he's my brother, Cormac concluded with a sigh. Because he *was* that little boy running at my side that I am never able to forget, though I try.

Well, and oh well . . .

Oh, it was a puzzle, a hard puzzle, this life on earth. Watching the grown-ups, he had little hope that it would get less so.

At least he wouldn't grow up to be a woman.

Enough, he thought. Enough of such thinking. Let's try to enjoy this day in spite of all.

As they neared the millrace, he lifted a quieting hand.

"Get down in this hollow here," he whispered, and they crouched, watching the swift-running water rush over the wheel, turning it steadily, as it moved the great stone quern within the mill, for the grinding of corn. It flowed in a thunderous cataract, splashing into the dark millpond.

"What are we doing?" Dal shouted over the roar of the water.

"Maybe nothing," Cormac replied. He hoped nothing. In a little while—and Dal, ever impatient, would not wait long—he could say that the expedition was a failure, and they'd go home, to forget about it. He could count on that, since Natt and Dal had queerly short memories, seemed to live entirely in the present, like Pangur Ban, or Mag, or any sheep.

But—here they came!

Two river otters, brown and sleek and shining, rippled up the path beside the millrace. Unaware of watching eyes, they raced and tumbled along the bank, intent on their game.

With a movement natural to him as breathing, Dal picked up a stone, and felt Cormac's hand clamp on his wrist, tight enough to be painful.

"*Drop it.*"

"You're hurting me, you fool clod!"

"Drop the stone."

Dal opened his fingers, let the stone fall, rubbed his wrist. "I wasn't going to harm them. I wouldn't harm an otter."

You'd harm anything that couldn't protect itself, Cormac thought, but held his tongue.

"Why'd you pick up the stone, atall?" Kerry said angrily. "I think Cormac's right. You should go for a soldier."

"Oh, should I, indeed? Then who'd be helping Da with the farm, so? You two?" Dal laughed. "We'd be reduced to cottiers in a year—"

"Oh, will you all hush!" Cormac said, ready to weep that he'd got himself and the otters into this situation.

"I didn't say one word," Natt offered. "Oh, look! Look, will you, at what they're after doing!"

Here they came, headfirst, down the rushing torrent, front legs held against their sides. Over the waterwheel they flew, and arced into the deep pond, disappearing from view.

The boys gazed in rapture. Never had they seen anything to match this. The joy of it stopped their quarreling, as side by side, in unspeaking bliss, they waited for the creatures to reappear.

Two large-eyed, whiskered brown heads surfaced, the otters swam to the rushy bank, clambered out to race up the return path and begin their watery journey over again.

For nearly an hour the pair continued their game. The boys would have watched all day, wordless, unwearying. But the otters seemed all at once to agree they'd had enough sport for now. One last ride and they swam to the opposite bank, flowed into the reeds, and disappeared.

Dal turned to Cormac. "That was the best thing I ever saw in me entire life. And I wouldn't tell, Cor. Never would I."

"I know," Cormac answered, then jumped to his feet, stripping off his clothes.

"If they can, we can!" he shouted.

He ran and leaped into the rushing stream, yelping as it carried him down and down, feet first, over the waterwheel, hurling him into the dark brown waters of the pond that still kept the chill of winter. After him came Kerry and Dal and Natt, hollering . . . wild with the joy of it.

Trudging home at midmorning, the brothers were as happily fond as ever they'd been in their lives before, or ever would be again.

CHAPTER VII

N A DAY in July, at first light, Hugh Boyle arrived with his wagon, his two oldest boys, Conall and Dermod, a lunch bucket, and their large mule, called Dandelion after a yellow spot on his ear.

Liam, with Cormac and Kerry, was waiting, a leather lunch bucket beside them. Lashed to a wooden sled was their curragh, a stout craft of hide stretched over an oak frame, built many years before by Liam and his own father. Cod nets were piled in the boat.

"God be with all in the house!" Hugh shouted, but none within replied, the women busy with the start of the day's work, and Dal and Natt, left out of the day's excursion, away in the pasture with Mag and the sheep.

Cormac had milked Jemmy and turned her out to graze. Kerry had fetched from the springhouse what his mother asked for, and now they were on their toes, tingling to be off. All day, all day by the sea! To fish, to gather cockles and mussels and—even Liam Brudair agreeing and taking part—to spend some useless, lazy, glorious time afloat on the waves.

"I don't see *why* we can't go," Dal had raged. "Why should we be left out and Cor and Kerry get to go?"

"You and Natt went last time," said Brudair. "There's not room in Boyle's wagon for all of you, so let's hear no more on it."

"I'm small." That from Meg. "I could fit."

No one paid her mind. Cormac, as he sometimes did of late, felt sorry for his sister. Though it was but three miles from this, Meg had never seen the ocean, nor was like to.

Had Gammer or his mother seen it? He'd never asked.

"I wonder," he said to Kerry, "if Mither or Gammer have been to the sea?"

But Kerry, nearly mindless with joy, did not hear.

Liam and Hugh attached the sled to the back of the wagon and they climbed on, boys in back, Liam beside his neighbor, who clucked to Dandelion and slapped the reins gently on the broad gray back.

They were off!

Along the lane, between hedgerows and windbreaks, then down a boreen that led from the lane, they rocked and rattled.

The other three boys chattered among themselves

of the grand fish they'd be catching, and the fine mussels they'd be eating tonight. Cormac listened to his father and Hugh Boyle, who were speaking, as they usually did, of burdens laid upon yeomen by the High Chiefs.

"Stands on the ridge of the world, so he thinks," Liam growled, speaking, of course, of the Ui Niall.

Hugh Boyle laughed. "Until he looks toward Tara and sees a ridge higher than his own."

"I doubt he turns his eyes in that direction, he's that busy looking in ours. Making sure we don't keep back a fleece, or the odd piece of kindling. Knows to a turnip our yield, robber that he is."

"Oh now," Boyle said indifferently. "It's as it always has been and will be. I don't hold with bucking against things as they are. Makes me stomach rumble."

"Neither does an ox buck. Do you see yourself in the light of an ox, so?"

"The Dear knows I work like one," Hugh said without rancor.

He's a strange fellow, Cormac thought. Is there nothing troubles him? What would it be like to have such a da, and he laughing, it seemed, at all that befell? Laughed at labor, at life itself, even at the unfairness of it—

"Look there!" Conall shouted, pointing down the road they'd come. "Look at Dal, how he's racing after us!"

"Whoa, Dandelion," said Boyle, pulling the mule to a stop.

Here came Dal, running like a hare, leaping stones

and ruts, gaining on them. He arrived at the wagon, breathing easily, smiling with delight.

"Is there something wrong at the house, then?" said Liam, for the moment not taking in that all Dal intended was to be taken along. "Speak up, lad!"

"No, no . . . nothing atall. I was just of a mind to go with you, and Mither said—"

"Your mother is altogether too easy with the lot of you. What about the sheep?"

"Mither said it didn't take two of us. She said—"

"It's no matter what she said. Back you go!"

Dal and the four boys in the wagon turned to Liam Brudair, staring in disbelief. Could it be that he'd send a fellow back who'd run all this way to join them?

Could even *he* be so hard? Cormac asked himself, half minded to hold out a hand and haul Dal into the wagon, but not entirely daring.

"Brudair," said Hugh Boyle, "you've a heart of flint, though I say it as should not."

"Should not, and will not—"

"I have already, and I'll say it again. Flint it is you've there in your breast. Let the lad in the wagon, man, that's run like a hero in a race."

"Please, Da?" Dal's face, upturned to his father's, had lost its look of joy for one of entreaty.

Kerry put a hand on his father's arm, saying, "It's a brave thing he's done, is it not—to catch us up on such a rocky road, Da? Sure, wouldn't it be the pity to turn him back now?"

Liam scratched his chin, looked about the air for answer.

"Climb on," he said gruffly, and faced forward.

"Hup, hup," said Hugh Boyle to his mule.

On they went, Dal grinning about, after making sure his father wasn't looking.

Sometimes Cormac felt that this brother of his was already completely the person he was intended to be, and nothing now would alter him, except that his body would grow. Dal wouldn't haver and waver, waiting for a *sign* to tell him he could do as he wished. Whatever Dal wanted—to be a farmer, a soldier, a High Chief itself should he be so minded, and Cormac would put nothing past him—Dal would assume that since it was what he wanted, why then God would see that he got it.

And were no sign given, would Dal think such was necessary? Not a bit of it. He'd decide that God's attention was elsewhere, and get on with his project single-handed.

"What about Natt?" Kerry asked.

"About him?" said Dal.

"How is it you got away from him?"

"He didn't know I was coming, atall. I didn't know it meself till I was half down the cowlane."

"He'll be angry."

Dal shrugged.

"You said you'd asked Mither and she gave you leave," Cormac pointed out.

"Did I, now?" Dal laughed and began to argue with Conall and Dermod about who could swim underwater the longest.

Da makes us lie, Cormac thought. He puts us in prison, and the only chink of escape we can find is the lie.

Doubtless his father was in the right of it, driving himself and the rest of them like mules, like Dandelion there. How else survive? But with Hugh Boyle for master, he went on to himself, I expect Dandelion makes out some better than we do.

He looked at the backs of the two men. Boyle was a huge fellow, with heavy shoulders and bushy hair. He was always humming or roaring or laughing or whistling, never quiet.

And me Da? Cormac asked himself. That hard-muscled man with skin stretched over his bones so tight you could almost know his skeleton?

How came these two to be friends?

The answer wasn't far to find. The Boyles and Brudairs were the only families close enough in the glen to visit back and forth. The families on outlying farms had their own small chapels for Sundays, and only came to the abbey on holy days—Easter and Christmas and special saints' days. Once a year, they all gathered at a great fair. Other than that, there was no meeting, no communication.

It's a lonely life, Cormac thought. And is all we have in common the work of the farm? All we have to talk about crops and weather and the Ui Niall?

Yes. That was all of it.

In the abbey, the rule of silence was observed. When taking fruit, vegetables, cheese, fleeces up to the monks, or when going into the laymen's part of the church for services, Cormac observed closely all that he could of the life up there. He watched the line of cowled brothers, hands in their sleeves, move slowly along the cloister toward "instruction," or toward their part of the church to observe the offices of the day.

The holy hours.

Prior Aelric had told him the beautiful names of these seven offices. Sometimes, lying sprawled with his brothers abed in the dark, he would say the words over to himself. . . .

Matins and Lauds at midnight. Prime just after sunrise. Terce between sunrise and noon. Sext, the sixth hour, midday. None, the ninth hour, about three o'clock. Vespers, next to the last of the canonical hours, called Evensong. And Compline, the last office of the day before bed, between eight and nine o'clock.

Dal, even Kerry, recoiled from the thought of a monk's life, could not abide the prospect of having to pray and listen to sermons, readings of scripture, of psalms, seven times every day. They blenched at the sight of the silent hooded brothers walking in line.

"But the singing," Cormac had said to them. "Don't you think the singing of the choir monks at Vespers is the most beautiful sound in the world?"

"Not me," Dal replied. "I'd rather hear a bobcat scream, or a lark sing in the sky."

"I'd rather hear Mither tell tales in the evening," said Kerry.

"And if the only time I could open me mouth was to chant in a church," Dal had gone on, "I'd go crazy." He'd lifted his voice and warbled, "Ah me, ah woe woe me . . . *culpa culpa mea culpa.*' Sure, and me voice is better nor the bobcat's scream would you not say—"

Cormac had to laugh. He, too, loved the voices of God's creatures . . . the lark, the bobcat, the stag belling on a distant hill. And, in the evening, when the wind went whistling down the glen and they in their snug cottage, in wavering rushlight, listened to their mother tell of heroes dead and gone, she chanting in *her* way, why, then he was happy as ever he thought to be in his life.

And yet—Evensong, in the trained voices of the choir monks—he had said once to Kerry that it seemed a strain that came direct from Heaven.

"I think," Kerry replied, "that Mither's voice is from Heaven, and so is a bird's song, or a wolf's cry. It's only what I think, but I think it."

Kerry was in the right of it. And Cormac could not explain why the voices of the monks seemed to melt his heart with the saddest kind of joy, of longing.

"Oh, look, Cor!" Kerry said now, pulling his brother's arm. "Look how they look—that sadly *poor.*"

The boreen had opened onto a wide shingly track. They were close enough now to the sea to inhale its briny, kelpy odor, and hear the surf ride up on the rocky shore.

Crouched in a hollow, backed for protection against a great sand dune, was a cottier's hovel, made mostly of withy sticks, with some attempt at wattle and daub. Running in and out and around the hut was a troop of half-naked children. Step-aged, bone-skinny, tangle-haired little savages they looked, and were all at once silent as they gazed at this passing wagon with its mule, its curragh, its well-fed passengers.

Dal sniffed. "Bunch of dirty little snarleyows."

"Dal," said Cormac. "You are not a nice person. I would not want you to be making the mistake of thinking you are."

"It's going to trouble me dreams, it is, that you should say such a frightening thing to me." Dal clutched his breast, made as if to draw out a dagger. "Indeed, it's such a wound as I may never recover from."

"I only thought I'd tell you what I think."

"As if you had need to tell me. Now I'll tell what I think of you and your moony monkish dafty ways...."

"Leave off, the both of you," Liam Brudair said over his shoulder.

The cottier children had run forward to surround the cart, holding up dirt-encrusted scabby arms, shrieking all together.

"Give us a bit o' bread, me lords," they cried. "A morsel o' cheese, for the love of God!"

"Drive on," Liam said crossly.

"Agh, you wouldn't be asking me not to stop and give them a wee share of our lunch, now?" Hugh Boyle pulled Dandelion to a halt and turned toward the back of the wagon. "Lads, get out a loaf and some'at of cheese and give them a jug of that cider there, we've plenty to sustain us."

Conall and Dermod were already rooting around in the leather lunch bucket. They leaned over the wagon,

71

handing over a loaf, a round of cheese, some apples, and the jug.

The largest two or three of the waifs grabbed and ran, pursued by the others in tears.

Liam Brudair shook his head. "Animals. Like animals at a kill. And are you thinking, Boyle, to be thanked, or to lay eyes on that pottery jug again?"

"Probably not," said Hugh. "We have other jugs. As to thanks—they're hungry, not grateful."

"Well, if you have food and good jugs to throw about, I have not."

"In that case," said Boyle, clucking to Dandelion who started foward again, "let us hope me lads gave of our own food and none of yours, Liam Brudair. It's short shrift the Savior Himself would get from the likes of you should He come in rags."

"You've no call to be judging of how I'd behave toward the Savior. As if I wouldn't be able to tell between Him and a tribe of rascally spalpeens."

"Maybe," said Boyle. "And maybe not."

They went on in silence, the boys looking at one another dismally, wondering how the day would be now, and their fathers at odds again this way.

CHAPTER VIII

NIGHT OF gust-driven rain. That sort of night when Gammer had claimed Druid spirits returned, trying to take Ireland back from Christ. Lightning skated down the sky, followed by the oaken rumble of thunder. This was not the gracious showers to which they were accustomed, but a rampage that had made a lake of the croft, from which even the geese had fled to shelter in the barn.

The wind, finding no entry at door, sides, or thatch, lunged down the smokehole, set the peat fire smoldering, tossed lantern shadows about the room.

It had been a long day, and after all, in most ways, a good day, Liam and Hugh Boyle making their peace as they always did, fearing a rift that would go too far, leaving each family isolated.

And it is not, Cormac thought, only for company's sake that we daren't risk a feud, but for the assurance that should need be, we will help one another in times of peril or sadness.

There was safety and solace in friendship.

They had rowed the curragh out on a low-waved sea, spreading their net in a circle, and taken four large cod, enough to salt down and serve for many winter meals. They had pried with stout knives two bucketsful of cockles and mussels.

They had shed their clothes and floated on the lifting and falling waves. Cormac, closing his eyes, thought he could still feel the gentle cradling of the sea, still hear the cry of cliff-nesting seabirds that wheeled overhead, soaring and diving as they, too, went about the day's fishing.

Sleepily, he listened now to his mother's singsong recital of "The Cattle Raid of Cooley."

" 'Oh, by my arms and my valor,' shouted Cuchulainn, 'I will have this Bull of Cooley and fifty heifers besides in despite of Ferdiad son of Daman son of Daire, horn-skinned and valiant though he be, and I swear that I will take him limb from limb and have out his eyeballs and strike off his head before I put one foot in retreat before him. . . . in all my life I have not turned in flight before one man nor before a multitude of men, nor shall I this day. . . .' Thus spoke Cuchulainn, holding straight

74

*before his face the three-ridged battle sword
and swearing mightily so that all trembled to
hear his oaths..."*

Irish kings and Irish chiefs, Cormac said to himself.
Have they ever done aught but fight and blather and
brag and bellow battle cries through the woods like
any stag?

Did they or do they care for aught but war, the
hunt, oaths, boasts of their valor?

Once he had asked his mother why she did not
sing of kind men, of good men.

"You could give us the tale of Saint Columba,
Mither, who sailed to Iona with the Word. Or of Saint
Patrick, who was brought to this island a slave from
Britain and put to tend swine and escaped and was
ordained priest and returned here to tell us, who did
not know, of Jesus and the saints and—"

"Cormac," his mother replied. "I sing only the tales
I have learned. There's no power in me to be making
up histories."

"Sure, and why not? You use words to tell of kings
and border battles, why not words that speak of saints?
Or—could you not yourself make up stories? Sing
about such as us—yeoman farmers that time out of
memory have kept full the bellies of the chiefs so they
can spend their time howling about how brawny and
brave they are. Would that not be the grand thing, to
sing of the men of the glen? Even the women," he
had added boldly.

"We are not the stuff of ballads, Cormac, and I

75

know but the words I know." She had smiled and put a gentle hand on his head. "Where you get your notions from, the Dear only knows. I do not think," she added with a sigh, "that they are the notions of a yeoman farmer."

She had added, surprising him, "One day, when your father is away, could you not bring me one of the pictures you've told me of? The way I could know what it is you are doing, if I could see such a picture, for a moment. You could take it back then to wherever it is you go—when you escape from us."

"I would like to, Mither. I would like to give you the best of them to put up on the wall."

"Put up on the wall?" she asked, puzzled. "I never— why would I—On the *wall*? Here, in the cottage? Why?"

"To look at, Mither. To have something pretty to look at sometimes, during the day. I have one of a field mouse and a weed that I am almost proud of. Nothing is ever quite what I have in me mind, though."

"A field mouse? A weed? Cormac, I cannot fathom what you are or wish to be and I wonder sometimes what is to become of you when I'm gone. This I do know—your father will have no picture put up on the *wall*. He'd think you dafty, and me as well."

Now Cormac leaned against a wall where the only pictures were restless shadows, and stroked Pangur Ban, purring on his lap with a husky sound, like that of the peat fire.

What indeed was to become of him when his mother, long life to her, was gone. Who would stand between him and his father? Who would accept, without having to understand, that his notions were not those of a farmer? Who would understand without prying that he needed, sometimes, to "escape" from the rest of them.

He dismissed the swaggering threats of Cuchulainn, and thought back to this past day by the sea.

In the afternoon, when they had fished and swum till even Dal, the tireless, was ready to take his rest, they had feasted on bread and cheese, cockles and apples and onions and cider. The same food, except for the cockles, and more of it, that they would take for the midday meal at home or in the fields.

Why did it taste so different—so savory—when eaten on a strand where the waves came riding ashore in long combers touched with sea frets, and the seabirds cried from their cliffside aeries?

Why was he always happiest away from the farm?

He had picked up a stick and drawn an angel in the sand.

"What's that?" Dal had said, appearing suddenly in that way he had. Like an apparition, Cormac thought nervously, making to scratch out his drawing, finding he could not.

"It's an angel," he'd said, sounding gruff, almost like his da.

"An angel, is it? You are drawing an *angel* with yer own hand with a stick? How come you to do that?"

He turned and shouted, "Da! Come here! Come and see what Cormac is after doing here in the sand with a stick!"

Cormac sat tight-lipped, cursing himself for a feckless reckless fool. To draw this, when all the years he had kept his secret, had had this one thing to himself. It was the sand tempted him. He'd found it so easy, to draw in the sand.

They crowded round, the lot of them, Cormac crouched in the middle beside his drawing, wishing he'd drowned earlier on. He could be this minute at peace at the bottom of the waves with the fish, spared the curiosity, the puzzlement, of all these people.

Spared his father's bewildered anger.

"It has six wings, begob," said Hugh Boyle. "That's an odd thing, Cormac, me lad. Whoever heard of an angel with six wings?"

"It's crazy," said Dal.

"It's beautiful," said Conall Boyle and Kerry together.

Cormac said sulkily, "There's two wings to cover her face and two to cover her feet and two to fly with."

"Well, I never in all me born days—" Hugh began, but was interrupted.

"What do you mean, *her*?" Liam demanded. "Angels are men!"

Hugh Boyle scratched his chin. "Well now, Brudair, we can't be sure of that entirely, not having seen, so to speak, any personal angels. Unless by chance you have, your own self, had a visitation?"

"Chop the natter, Boyle. God made angels and he

made them *men*. Look at your Gabriel, and your Michael, and—" Liam stopped, strangled with coughing.

"Your Satan," Boyle said, when the fit was past.

"That's right. He was an angel, until he fell."

"And afterward, too. An angel still, after the Fall."

"That has nothing—" Liam began, clenched his jaw and his fists and glared about. "What we've to do with here is what this—this boy of—of mine—is up to with his—with this drawing of angels. How comes he to be doing such a thing atall and I doubt not it's sacrilege—"

"Why?" asked Boyle. "Those High Crosses at Kildare have angels chiseled in them. For the matter of that, Christ Himself is on them or why would they be after calling them crosses, so why should Cormac not feel free to draw one." He studied the lines in the sand. "Six wings, though. How did he ever think of that?"

Clouds were piling up, building one upon the other. A sandy breeze began to blow the picture away. Cormac took up his stick and erased what was left before racing with the rest for the wagon.

When they came to the cottier's hovel, Hugh Boyle pulled up Dandelion. This time the cottier himself came to the doorway, scowling. He had the cider jug in his hand. "What reason have you to stop here?" he demanded.

Brudair looked at Boyle with the same question in his eyes.

"We—I mean, I—" Hugh said to the man, "have this extra cod here you might use—"

The man took a step forward, brushing children out of his way. "We want none of yer leavings. Here's the jug you left. Take it and begone."

"Leavings, is it?" Boyle shouted at him. "This is a grand fresh cod not an hour out of the sea."

"You can put it back in the sea, for all of me."

Behind him, his thin wife stood wringing her hands while the children howled and wept, reaching their hands toward the fish.

"Fool!" Boyle said angrily. "You think only of yerself then?"

"My business what I think. Get along with you—yer *lordship.*"

They moved on, followed by the desolate cries of the children.

"It's your fish and your foolishness," said Brudair. "And nothing of mine."

"True, true," Boyle replied. "I had to try."

"He scorned you."

"That is also true."

"You'd think for his children's sake—"

"A prickly-proud man who leaves his children's bellies empty that might this once have been filled. They run away from him, as soon as they're old enough. But more keep coming."

"Run away?" Cormac spoke up. "How so? They are cottiers, they belong to the Ui Niall. How can they run?" At Boyle's shrug, he pressed on, "Doesn't he send after them, so? They being his property, like field beasts?"

"If a field beast is a starveling, and sickly, he does

80

not send after it. He lets it wander at will, die where it may."

Boyle slapped the reins on Dandelion's back, dismissing Cormac and his questions. They went on in silence, glancing at the sky as if to hold the storm off with the looking.

At the stone steps leading up the cliff to the monastery, Boyle again drew Dandelion to a stop.

"Well, and what is it now?" Brudair demanded.

"I'm just going to take this bucket of mussels and cockles up to the brothers, they'll be that glad of something fresh."

"The rain is coming on!" Liam protested. "Take the things up tomorrow, will you not? Why now, for the love of Jesus?"

"Now's me choice," said Hugh, adding, "So long as I'm up there, I'll be taking a moment to confess to Father Aelric—"

Liam Brudair let out a howl of rage. "Begob, Boyle! Won't yer sins keep till Sunday?"

Climbing down from the wagon, Boyle shouldered a bucket, patted Dandelion, and walked off, saying over his shoulder, "The rain'll hold off—see if I'm not right."

Red-faced, shaking with fury, Liam hunched over, big hands hanging between his knees. His breath came in noisy snorts, and for a while the boys behind him dared not speak.

Desperately wanting permission to go with Hugh Boyle, Cormac held his tongue as he gazed after the farmer's climbing figure. In a moment, he would be there, on the sacred plateau, privileged to speak with, look into the eyes of, Father Aelric. Perhaps even Abbot Maher himself.

Dal, looking up at the wall surrounding the abbey buildings, turned to his older brother.

"That's going to be your home, Cor. I see it plain. It's not long till you'll be living up there. Praying for us sinners. It's where you should be." He sounded serious, almost gentle.

Cormac had looked at him sideways. Was this the sign? That the brother who held him in contempt should suddenly speak so softly, with such assurance? Dal, the inheritor, maybe, of Gammer's prophesying tongue?

He wanted to say, How do you know? He wanted to ask, Are you sure? He dared not. Something so fragile, so yearned for, as this forecast of the life he might one day come to, could be shattered by a word, surely. Destroyed by a touch of doubt.

He put out his hand and clasped lightly, in silence, the hand of his brother.

The storm held off until they neared the Brudair farm, when a wind began to trouble the trees, and rain in great drops to pit the dust of the lane.

"Jesus, Mary, and Joseph," Hugh Boyle roared, "we'll be drenched like sheep in a meadow before we make home. If we are not speared by the lightning itself."

"Well, you're shriven," Liam said crossly. "What

82

better time to be struck down than when fresh to a state of grace?"

"I did not get to see the priest at all, didn't you know?"

As they'd not exchanged a word from there to this, it was no surprise that none of them knew.

"Well. You can take shelter in the barn until the worst of it passes," Liam said, and added grudgingly, "I'd offer the house, but we'd smother all together, so—"

"No, no. We'll press on, won't we lads?" Hugh said to his sons, who agreed merrily.

Almost asleep now, Cormac wondered whether they were home yet. If they were not, he could hear them laughing in the rain, the way Hugh Boyle always had his boys laughing.

He brooded over the sheep in the pasture, the way they'd be huddled together, bleating in this downpour the likes of which not one of them had ever known till this. He wondered about those starveling cottier's children in their stick hut that surely the rain would have easy entry to and would put out their fire if they had one.

Sometimes he felt he could hardly bear it, how animals had to endure in silent patience all that was visited upon them. How children—and grown people, too, who were luckless—had to take the ills that befell them, with no way, nowhere, to turn for help.

"There is God to turn to," he could hear the abbot

say reproachfully. But, if the cottiers of the glen did indeed pray, it seemed certain that through some ill luck their beseeching voices did not ascend to Heaven, went unheard, had always gone unheard.

We are lucky, he mused, stroking Pangur. Safe, with a sturdy house, with good food. And *free*, not like that cottier and his wild brood, living in that hovel of withes, and even those not their own, and themselves owned by the Ui Niall, he caring no more for them than for a sick beast.

Hugh Boyle said no man need clamor against fate who owned his own roof and the land about it. "I'll give the Ui Niall what is due him, and no more. I'll bow no more to him than he to me," said Boyle, jutting his chin.

Cormac thought of his father, dragging his cap off under the steward's imperious gaze. He had no doubt that Hugh Boyle, for all his high claims, submitted to that unspoken bidding, that sneer of command.

Boyle was a man who did not look for trouble, and who'd fault him for that? Or for his boasts? Surely it took a measure of bluff to offset gestures of humility forced upon the men of the glen by the lords of the castle. Or how keep self-regard at all?

I do not think, Cormac said to himself, that Abbot Maher, or Prior Aelric, or the least brother of the abbey bows to the Ui Niall. He's too in need of their prayers, the way he lives.

" 'I swear by my arms of valor, by my leather buckler, by my silver three-ridged sword, that I

84

will pierce his body through and hear his dying
shriek and rejoice at it!' cried mighty Cuchu-
lainn—"

His mother sang the ancient lay, and the wind and the rain and grumbling thunder made a background to her voice. Cormac, weary of Irish heroes that seemed to him bladders of gas, thought of that cottier today and of the family he let starve to save his pride. Did they have any rags save what they wore? Anything warmer, or wool, to put on, come winter? He did not think so. Were they always hungry? He thought so.

Once, after making his confession to Prior Aelric, he had said boldy, "I want to ask a question, Father."

"Of course, Cormac."

"It's this, then—why does God, if He's so good, let some people grow fat and rich and leave others to starve and die in the cold? Why do some men, and not good men all, *have* all, when others lack a very shawl against the cold? I don't speak of meself, Father," he hurried on. "I have no cause to rail, I think God has been good to me, but *why* to me? Why—"

Prior Aelric had held up his hand in a priest's mildly commanding gesture. "Cormac, do you not think God is grieved at the way we misuse the gift He gave us, the gift of free will that sets us apart from the beasts? Had He known how flawed, how headstrong and self-willed and selfish and—and cruel—human beings would become, the powerful oppressing the frail, the canny deceiving the tender-witted—perhaps He would have thought again before allowing us so *much* self-

85

rule. But what God has granted, He cannot take back. Cormac, I think the heart of God breaks as he watches us—the imperfect beings that He hoped to create perfect."

Often, since, he had thought of the priest's words, which seemed to him beautiful—and not an answer to his question.

All at once he became aware that his mother had left off the chant.

"Children, to bed. It's late and I'm that tired and so must we all be. This storm will give us work enough to do tomorrow."

Cormac put Pangur Ban gently on the floor, and got to his feet. "I'll go to the barn and see if Jemmy is all right. Sometimes she minds the storms, which is not good for the milk."

"Do that," said his father. "Then come back and be ready to listen to me. I have some'at to say to you."

CHAPTER IX

ORMAC LINGERED in the barn, running his hand down Jemmy's flank. She seemed placid, unaffected by the elements, though at times, in a storm less wild than this, she became edgy, moving restlessly in her halter. Who would suppose a cow to have humors? Their Jemmy had.

"You're a good beast, a sweet beast," he said softly.

Jemmy flicked an ear and lowed as if in response, and Cormac, for all his apprehension, smiled at that.

"What do you suppose," he went on, "I have done now, that Himself has 'some'at' to say to me?" He plundered his mind, retrieving the day, and arrived at the angel in the sand.

Belike it had angered his da more than he'd let on before the others. Why? Because of the six wings?

Because he'd said the angel was a woman? That he'd drawn it at all? What harm to trace a few lines that would shortly be washed away or blown away?

No use to try reason. It wasn't the lines in the sand that had his da in another taking. More troublous than that, surely.

Had it been blasphemy—he sinning in a way he had not understood and must pay for. In what coin? He did not think even a hard switching would suffice.

"Cormac!" His father's voice, lifted above the storm. "Get in here! Now!"

Drawing a quick breath, he splashed over the croft to the cottage and stood, heart thudding, looking no higher than his father's boots. His mother was in the room, her eyes wide and tearfilled. Gammer in her corner was asleep. The children had been sent to bed.

This is the worst that has ever happened, Cormac thought. He is going to say something terrible that will never be unsaid, and what's to become of me now? He shifted his glance for a moment to his mother's face, but she'd turned away, one hand to her mouth, the other twisting her shawl.

"I have decided," said Brudair, "that you and I will go to the abbey tomorrow and ask Father Maher to take you in."

Cleft by an inward tremor, near swooning, Cormac tried to speak, and found no voice. Here it was, what he had longed for, prayed for, and he wanted to cry out, "No! I cannot leave here, where is everything, everyone I know. I am *afraid* to leave here...."

He looked at his mother, her face still turned away. She could wheedle and sometimes charm her husband, in small matters. They none of them had defense against Liam Brudair when he'd set his mind.

The stern, steady voice continued. "You will never make a farmer. Dal is—" He stopped, unable to describe how superior was the younger brother to him now addressed. "You are fit for nothing, or next to nothing, here with us. If the abbey will have you, and I'll be after telling Abbot Maher about your gormless ways, naught else would be honest—but if they will take you and teach you these—teach you to *read*, and to *write*"—in the midst of his terror and confusion, Cormac yet had time to think that his father might have been saying "to lie" and "to steal," so deep was his scorn of the cloistered way, for all he reverenced the cloistered men.

"If they will have you, there'll you stay. Here—the truth on it is you do not earn your keep."

A sob escaped his mother's lips. Unheeding, Liam continued stonily, "What all this—this drawing of angels means is not in my power to tell. It may be ungodly. I know naught about such matters. Neither do I know what you are about when you shirk your duty and disappear in the woods and ignore my calls. But you'll never make a farmer," he said again, and could not say worse.

"In the morning," he went on, "milk Jemmy. If it has stopped raining, turn her out to graze. Then you and I will go up the hill and get this settled. One way or the other way. If you are refused, you will start to

89

do your share of the work of this farm. There'll be no more sneaking off with your mother's weak-minded yea. And no more drawing of—of things. You'll be a farmer, you'll act like one and work like one. That's all about it. Get to bed."

Lying on his pallet next to Kerry, Pangur Ban asleep between them, Cormac stared into the dark—wakeful, afraid, hopeful.

If Abbot Maher should say there was room in the abbey for a lad who had set his heart on learning—what then? Would he ever see Kerry again, or his mother?

And would he not leave them? In heartache, but not looking back? He would, he knew well that he would. He wondered, listening to the rain, now only a rustling in the thatch, if he was not only not the stuff of which farmers were made, but a worthless brother and son besides.

A gormless calf, entirely.

Yet now that the threat had been made—and his da would see it as no other than a threat—he began to feel a low thrill in his body, a humming of hope rather like the throbbing purr of Pangur Ban.

He pulled the cat onto his chest, smoothed the soft fur, and tried to communicate a silent understanding. If they would accept him up there on the hill and take Pangur Ban, too, how happy he would be. But—should the answer be yes to him and no to Pangur—"Why then," he whispered to the purring beast, "you will remain here, part of this life and no part of mine. I cannot do else. I cannot."

The next morning, in a world running with brown freshets, he and his father mounted the steep stone steps cut in the cliff that led to the abbey and inquired of the porter at the gate for Abbot Maher.

The abbot himself received them, and for him Liam Brudair willingly pulled his cap off, even jerked his forelock slightly.

"I've brought me son here to you, Father, to leave here, if you'll have him."

"An oblate," said the abbot. "I see."

"Oblate, yer honor? I don't know as how—"

"A son, or daughter, offered to the Church by parents, is called an oblate, Liam Brudair."

"So be it," said Brudair. He turned, as if to get on with his business, but realized the matter was far from concluded, and stayed.

"So, Cormac," said Abbot Maher. "You think that you wish to come here and live our hard and holy life, leaving behind your family and all that you have known till this."

"Yes, Father Abbot. I do wish it. I want to take my vows and learn everything—" He broke off at his father's beetling frown.

"As to vows," Abbot Maher went on, "That would be a long way off, my son, even should you be admitted here. You do not announce that you wish to learn everything and thereby assume you will prove able or worthy to learn anything. If we take you, you will be an oblate, not a novice for some time yet. And we have novices who've been with us for years, still not judged ready for the tonsure and final vows."

"But I'll try! I'll do anything!"

"You feel you have a call to God?"

Cormac, falling silent, looked at the floor with a sense of entire loss. He could not say he had a call. Or, he had one, but not to God. Not yet. Only a call to learning.

It was not going to be enough.

He looked from the abbot to his father and back. "No, Father," he said. "I *wish* to feel that. I have prayed for it. But the call does not come. I keep seeking a sign, and yesterday when me brother Dal said one day I would live up here, I thought maybe that was it—and then when me da said I'm no use on the farm—"

Brudair interrupted. "I suppose this is as good a lad, in his nature," he said truculently, almost reluctantly, "as any of yer chief's sprouts that you take in up here will or nill—"

"No." The abbot was tranquil. "All boys are considered equally."

Brudair, looking skeptical, went on. "I must tell you, further, not being a man to misrepresent, that this here is bone-lazy, and getting a proper day's work out of him—short of beating, which I do not altogether hold with—is the near side of impossible. Gormless I've called him, gormless he is, and that's the truth on it." Liam Brudair drew a breath. This was more speech from him than Cormac had heard before, and it appeared he was not finished yet. "So I said to meself that maybe up here at the abbey he'd be forced to do a day's work even though what he's always on about is learning letters—a useless fritter for a farmer's son—"

Years later, Abbot Maher told Brother Cormac that it had been that speech, and the expression of helpless despair that Cormac turned upon him, that decided the matter.

"I could no more have turned away a legless beggar than you, who seemed all at once to have no legs at all to stand upon."

"Thank God," Cormac whispered. "Thank you, beloved Father."

That first day, the abbot said to Liam Brudair, "I am minded to give your son a chance with us. If he can live by the Rule, can adapt himself to a severe life, and if he can contribute to our community in some fashion—we will give him time to find his niche—why then, we will receive him. Otherwise—"

"Otherwise he comes back to me farm and sheds his idle ways and dafty doings—" For a moment, his son knew, Brudair was on the point of describing the six-winged angel in the sand, but found the words too bitter to form. He said, "That's all about it, Father. I'll be saying good-bye, with your blessing."

When the porter closed the gate, Liam Brudair was outside, and Cormac within.

"Forever, dear God, should it please You," he said, in a silent prayer. "But Thy will be done."

He added, almost immediately, "Please, Father Abbot, may I have my cat, Pangur Ban, with me here?"

"Your cat, is it?"

There was a long silence before the abbot spoke.

"You will need to get accustomed to much that is strange to you, Cormac. To sparser meals even than you've known, to monotonous days and interrupted nights, to work that you will not be permitted to shirk, gormless though you may be. I do not take your father's word for that. We shall see for ourselves."

Cormac thought of pointing out that his meals could scarcely grow sparser, that the monotony of life on the farm could scarcely be matched, that he cared not a whit for uninterrupted sleep, that he wanted only to work till he dropped in order to be worthy of life here on the hill within these walls.

"The monastic life," Abbot Maher continued, "is not, as you seem to picture it, one simply of learning. It is austere, a life of prayer, contrition, self-denial. Of humility and labor, *Ora et labora*. Pray and work. The Rule of Saint Benedict. It is also, for those chosen, a life of happiness and peace of spirit. But you must understand that in this house of God, we own nothing. No one says, 'My.' There is no *meum et tuum* here. All is God's."

Cormac cried out with delight, "You're speaking Latin to me!"

"I am. And it means that there is no mine and thine in the abbey. So when you say may you have *your* cat, I must of course reply, you may not have *your* anything."

Drawing a breath, Cormac said carefully, "But Father, nobody owns a cat. People only think that they do. That way he wouldn't be mine at all, you see, once he came here."

"You are a casuist, Cormac. Prior Aelric and I have noted that tendency in you."

"I don't know what it is, Father Abbot," said Cormac, eager to find out.

"A casuist is one who can turn and twist a question till it yields to his own meaning. I rather enjoy such disputations, and welcome the prospect of more. In time. Not immediately. Meanwhile, Brother Bernard, our novice master, will take you in hand. Do you know what the rule of silence is?"

"I—you don't talk?"

"We do not observe the rule as strictly as the great orders of the eastern coast, or those of Britain. Still, unnecessary chatter, or gossip of any sort, is proscribed. Ah." He looked up. "Here is Brother Bernard now, master of novices, told of your arrival by the porter, no doubt. Go with him."

"Father Abbot—my—I mean, *the* cat?"

Abbot Maher smiled briefly. "Gormless, perhaps. Stubborn, certainly." He turned to the elderly monk at his side. "Shall we have this cat, Bernard? Once the possession of Cormac here?"

"Brother Ceil kept that speckled goat as his particular creature," said the novice master. "It continues to provide us with excellent cheese, though Brother Ceil, God rest him, is no longer with us. Perhaps the cat will be a welcome ratter."

"Oh, yes," said Cormac. "That he is. Fearsome among the rats."

"Then it will be acceptable to welcome—what did you say his name is?" the abbot asked.

"Pangur Ban."

"A good name. We'll send for him. Now, go with Brother Bernard, who will show you as much as may be before Sext. You will attend the hour and with him, and High Mass following."

Cormac felt that he might melt for very joy. To attend the hour, and all the hours to come. To hear Mass, not, as before, in the lay person's part of the church, but in the company of the cloistered. And every day from this! Father Maher, his own father too, might question if he could abide by the rule, work in a way to prove himself not gormless—but he had no doubt in the world at all. Here he was, here he would remain ... enfolded, with this life spread before him, a field of blessedness. ...

"Oh, God—I thank you, I thank you. Make me worthy," he called silently. "Let my life here be forever worthy, amen."

The priest and the monk waited a moment in the presence of unspoken prayer.

CHAPTER X

ORMAC WAS never able to judge the age of grown people. Brother Bernard was many years younger than Gammer, older than his father, much older than Prior Aelric. Still, he was an old man.

And isn't it the wonder how briskly he walks, thought the boy, matching his stride to the monk's.

"Can I talk?" he asked.

"May you. Of course you may."

"But the rule—"

"This is your first day, almost your first minute, in the community. We'll not trouble about the rule until I have shown you about abbey and grounds and explained your duties. That done, we'll see you into a novice's habit. As you are our sole oblate, you will be more comfortable dressed like the others. We have, at

97

present, eight novices. Besides Abbot Maher and Father Aelric—priests, as you know—there are twenty-three brothers."

Cormac quivered. A habit! He was to wear the hooded homespun novice's garment, as one day, God willing, he would wear that of a professed monk. Even now, he would walk in procession cowled, with hands in his sleeves, and hear Mass in the monks' section of the church, and have his sleep interrupted by the holy hours—

"The Rule," Brother Bernard was saying, "does not consist merely of restraint in speech. It encompasses all that we do here. All that we refrain from doing. You will find, Cormac, if you remain with us, that there is not an hour of the day that is your own. Not one hour," he repeated, with a downward glance.

Cormac met the stern gaze gladly.

"There are the canonical hours to be observed, seven times daily—"

"I know them," Cormac interrupted. "Prior Aelric told them me when I asked, long ago, when I saw the procession of the brothers in the cloister and heard the choir monks singing. Oh, surely the angels in Heaven itself do not sing more beautifully than the monks in—in our abbey," he said, dazzled by his own daring.

"Son. I said you might talk. I should have said, you may listen. Ask questions. You've not been given leave to ramble on to no point."

"But—"

98

Brother Bernard lifted a hand. Assured that Cormac had taken his meaning, he continued. "You have, this morning, missed Lady Mass and chapter—"

Cormac could not refrain. "What is chapter, Brother Bernard?"

"A meeting of the entire community, at which the daily business of the Order is discussed—novices take no part in the discussion. The duties of the day are announced, after which we confess our faults publicly, and undertake correction."

"Confess *publicly?*"

"Inner transgressions are for your confessor, who will continue to be Father Aelric. Open defects call for public admission and chastisement."

"Brother Bernard—what is an open defect?"

"Gossiping, grumbling, indolence, prying, criticizing, petulance, shirking—unfortunately even in a community devoted to praising God and doing His work and His will, the list is overlong."

Cormac opened his mouth, but Brother Bernard swept on.

"There follows a reading from the psalms, and Father Abbot preaches a sermon. Then dinner, preceded by a visit to the lavatorium. There is no conversation at the midday meal, during which one of the senior monks reads from the refectory pulpit—homilies, or some portion from the lives of the saints. At mixtum, however—a slight collation taken after Prime—you may speak softly to the brothers to either side of you. After the noonday meal, you may walk for a

99

quarter of an hour in the cloister or the garth. A low exchange of words with your fellow students is permissible."

Students? Cormac thought, but did not ask, for fear Brother Bernard meant learning not Latin and letters, but the routine of the cloister.

"After Sext, when the refectory has been cleared, the cottiers and their families come for their daily meal. As at our own dinner, the novices take turns serving, and so shall you. The cottiers then visit Brother Francis, our infirmarer, should any be ailing."

"You feed the cottiers and their children every day?" said Cormac in wonder. "And see to their ills? I didn't know that."

"There is much you will learn about us. If you remain."

He glanced down, as if expecting a protest.

"There follows the list of daily assigned duties, and then None. After that—" The monk blew out a breath. "Do not attempt, Cormac, to learn all in a day. You will become part of our discipline here, seasoned to it—if it is meant to be. Of that we cannot yet be sure."

I can be sure, Cormac thought.

They had walked out of the cloistered arcade, across the grassed garth, around the four sides of which were the abbey buildings.

Largest and finest was the stone-built church, with its square bell tower. Next to it, part stone, part timber, was the refectory, a long room with two long wooden tables, benches to either side, a pulpit against the east wall, and on the wall itself a large painting of Christ upon the cross. Cormac and Brother Bernard remained a moment in silence, gazing at it.

"We'll go on, now," said the monk.

Adjoining the refectory was the lavatorium, where the monks washed at stone troughs fed by rainwater from an overhead stone cistern. Above refectory and kitchen was the dorter, where all members of the community slept.

"Father Abbot and Father Aelric sleep in the dorter with the rest of us. Each has a private cell at the far end. You will have no audience with them except by my leave, save when confessing to Prior Aelric. We hold chapter in the parlor, which is also used, by special dispensation, for a novice or monk to receive a visitor. In addition, parlor is where we relax the rule of silence for a half hour before Compline, the last hour before we retire."

"Brother Bernard—where is the scriptorium? Can I see where the books are? Can I look at the books?"

"Cormac. You clearly have much to learn. When you say *can* you look at the books, I answer that undoubtedly you are physically capable of looking at them. You have your eyesight. If you mean *may* you look at them, meaning will I permit you to, that is for the future. And this will go the easier if you do not interrupt. I have much yet to tell you and Sext is in less than an hour."

"I'm sorry, Brother Bernard. I'll try to do better."

"Do so. For two hours each morning you will take instruction from me, along with the other novices, in letters and Latin."

Cormac's heart leaped, but he tightened his lips against speech. It seemed to him that though Brother Bernard spoke much of the rule of silence, he was not averse to letting his own tongue wag.

He thought in dismay that already he had committed a transgression. No—two. Criticizing. Grumbling. How could he criticize or grumble at this good brother who was taking such patient pains with him, and who had spoken for Pangur Ban's admission?

Wrong of him, sinful, to be after finding fault with any person—but of the man who was to be his teacher! Ashamed, he gave his attention back to his guide, and tried to give it fully.

"Each day's duties," the monk continued, sounding tired, "are assigned, by me, to each novice. We have many duties, and arduous. There are the grain fields and corn and pease fields in the valley, which are worked in season. Up here there is the constant repair of the walls, the daily scrubbing of all floors, there is carding, spinning, looming, the making of rushlights and mending of habits. Daily milking, churning, brewing. Pallets and habits are laundered monthly. There is the care of our altar treasures, though that holy duty is reserved for professed monks...."

He gazed about, drew another deep breath. "There is work in the kitchen, helping Brother Philip prepare the meals. Serving in the refectory is taken in turn. Each novice sleeps once a week in the infirmary, assisting Brother Francis, the infirmarer, with sick or dying brothers. Much of the work in the infirmary is onerous, and some of it disgusting. You will bear yourself with unwincing benevolence so as not to wound the feelings of ..."

Cormac's mind wandered, returned, drifted off again as they visited the various cloister buildings.

In the dairy, he saw to his delight that there were three cows, and for a moment, felt a twinge of longing for a cow in a barn down in the valley. He would not, he supposed, ever again see Jemmy. Would he see any of them down there again? His mother. Surely she and Kerry would come to church and they would gaze at one another—they from the lay side, he from the cloistered....

His heart was all at once sore, and his throat ached. He had to turn his head away, hiding from Brother Bernard a rush of hot tears.

The tour continued.

They looked into the buttery, where the abbey stores were kept. Bread, ale, cider, cheese, butter, vegetables, fruits. They stopped in workshops. Silent monks sat at spinning wheels and looms, fashioning their plain hooded habits, plaiting rope girdles. At cobblers' benches sandals and boots were being fashioned, and in a section of the large barn brothers carved furniture, carved the wooden trenchers from which all ate, the wooden mugs from which they drank.

Wordless and diligent, the labor of the abbey progressed in kitchen, bakery, granary, workshops, stable, and garden.

Through it all Cormac followed Brother Bernard, in a windmill of impressions.

At length, outside the garth, they arrived at the

infirmary, where Brother Francis met them at the door, one finger to his lips.

"Asleep, praise God," he whispered. "All three asleep now."

"How do they fare?" Brother Bernard asked softly.

Francis shook his head. "I fear we are losing Joseph. But God's will be done. And who is this, Bernard?" He fixed a mild eye on Cormac.

"An oblate, offered by his father. Cormac Brudair. He feels he has a vocation."

"Let us hope he is right." Brother Francis put a hand on Cormac's thick tangle of black hair, so gently that Cormac was emboldened to speech.

"Who is Joseph?" he asked.

"Brother Joseph was—is—one of our scribes. A learned man. An artist. He was copying a missal lent us by the abbey at Rosserk. Most beautiful work he was doing, now halted, and who knows whether one of the others in the scriptorium can continue where Joseph left off. But God's will be done," he said again, adding, "Welcome here, young man, to His service."

Cormac, who'd experienced a shudder of rapture at the words *scribe*, *missal*, *scriptorium*, bowed his head. He willed himself to silence, and burst out, "Could I see the missal? The one he was copying?"

"Well—" Brother Francis began, "I should think—"

"We'll take our leave," Brother Bernard interrupted sharply. He turned and strode back toward the gate. Cormac, with a glance over his shoulder at Brother Francis, ran in pursuit, expecting a rebuke that did not come.

Crossing the garth, Brother Bernard went up the outside steps to the dorter.

In the doorway Cormac halted and stared in amazement.

"What are those?" he asked, pointing.

"Those?" said the monk, for a moment astonished. "The cots?"

"They're off the *floor!*" said Cormac, who had slept on a pallet on the ground all his life, and all his brothers with him.

"Is there one for each person?" he asked, staring at the double row of cots that lined the long room, each with a blanket and a pillow.

Brother Bernard's expression softened. "Yes, Cormac. One for each. This," he said, walking to the third bed on the right-hand wall, "is yours."

"Mine," Cormac whispered.

The monk resumed his role. "At midnight the dorter bell will ring. You will awake, sit quietly, feet together on the floor, head cowled, praying in silence until I, with a lamp, lead the way down the night stairs to church, for Matins and Lauds. You may be sleepy, but you are not to fall asleep during the office."

I won't be sleepy, Cormac thought. Not ever. I shall be ever ready to rise and go down the night stairs to Matins and Lauds. I shall ever be ready to live here, and be dutiful, and do God's work and will, and one day, if it please Him, take up where a dying brother leaves off work on a *missal.*

Reading his mind, something Cormac was to find Brother Bernard adept at, the monk said, "As to your seeing the scriptorium, the books, the missal upon which Brother Joseph's work has been sadly broken off—I tell you once more and not again, that is for the future. You are overeager, a tendency that must be curbed. Restraint, modesty, patience—learn these. Then, when I judge meet— Now it is time for Sext."

Downstairs, Abbot Maher emerged from the church and fixed a keen eye on his new oblate's drawn face. Cormac had gone from exhilaration to weary confusion, at seeing and hearing so much in so short a time.

He felt drowned in Brother Bernard's voice, his guidance and admonitions, instruction and explanations.

"If I may reverse myself," said the abbot, "I think it would be best if Cormac did not attend Sext or Mass today."

"As you think best, Father," the gray-haired monk said. He too sounded tired but kept his shoulders back.

"Cormac," said Father Maher. "Go off by yourself. Take a walk along the cliffside and think. Think deeply about what you are doing—whether it is truly what you wish. Be alone with your thoughts, *and* your doubts. Come back in an hour, when we take our midday meal. Later today, you and I will talk."

Cormac bowed his head, turned to thank Brother Bernard, and moved away, across the garth, through the wicket of a gate that led to a wide meadow where sheep were grazing.

Monks, with their habits dropped to the waist, moved along the rows of a large garden, some weeding, some gathering vegetables—carrots, turnips, cabbages. They worked steadily. Not one looked up as Cormac passed.

He walked along the cliff's edge, leaving the cloister far behind. Here and there on the wide tableland were stone beehive huts, built centuries ago, in the time of Saint Patrick himself, by anchorite monks. These had lived each by himself in a stone shelter erected by his own hands. Self-exiled, eating what eggs they could take from the nests of cliff-dwelling seabirds and what they were able to raise in little gardens at their doorsteps, they had spent their solitary lives in prayer and penance.

Cormac stooped to peer in one of the huts and found to his surprise a stone plate lying on the floor. Was it left here years out of memory, by a solitary religious who'd died here alone and been buried by his brother hermits, paying more heed to him in death than they had in life?

At the cliff's edge, he stood looking down to the ocean where it tossed on the rocky shore. From here, it seemed soundless, almost motionless. As far out as he could see, to the blurred horizon, nothing moved but a few seals in the gray water, a few gulls in the gray air.

He knelt and tried to pray.

CHAPTER XI

ORMAC LAY awake in the dark, alone in bed, hands beneath his head.

Last night, at this time, in another life, he had been in the room with his brothers, and Gammer and Meg, with Pangur Ban warm and purring on his chest. Close by, in the front room, his parents had slept. He thought that perhaps his mother had not been sleeping. Was she sleeping now? He thought not. She was lying awake thinking of him, as he of her.

Here he was, where he'd longed to be, where, should it please God, he would spend his life. Existence on this high hill was not, as he had once pictured it, an easy life of peace and quiet and prayer. It would be a harder row to hoe than any he'd gone down, following Dal and his da, picking up stones, all those many years.

Eight novices, one oblate, twenty-three brothers were here in this room, and the abbot and prior in their cells at the far end. He was one of these, asleep, or pretending to sleep, in the dark dorter.

Was he lonely? Was he frightened or regretful? He couldn't tell.

Tired but sleepless, his thoughts tumbled with recollections of the day just past. Of Brother Bernard, his stern and tolerant guide. Of Abbot Maher's kindly aloofness, and Brother Francis's gentle manner, in which even the dying would surely take comfort.

He tried to summon up the faces of other monks that Brother Bernard had pointed out to him, attempted to put names to them. It was difficult, since in nearly every case, except that of the infirmarer, Brother Bernard had said, "You will have no occasion to speak to him." Indeed, he had spoken to no one except the novice lying in the bed next to his.

"What's your name?" the boy, a little older than himself, had asked, when they'd come up here after Compline.

"Cormac."

"Mine's Owen," said the other, and no more.

Did he miss Kerry's dear voice, his mother's loving tones, his da's rough tongue? Dal's churlish one? He was unable to tell. He simply lay, somewhat cold despite the warm clean blanket, and gazed toward the glow of the small lamp on a wall bracket at the head of the night stairs. He listened to the call of a hunting owl, the bark of a fox, the rustle of a branch against the window over his head.

Deep steady breathing came through the dark. Stirrings, snores, shiftings.

Was everyone save himself asleep?

Was anyone else awake, weeping in silence—for someone, for someplace—now forever out of reach?

Did *he* want to cry, for Kerry, for his mother, for his little white cat?

He sat up, astonished that he could have forgot how Abbot Maher had promised Pangur Ban would be brought up from the glen to be, if not his own any longer, at least here where he was....

"Is aught amiss, Cormac?"

It was Brother Bernard, leaning over him, speaking softly. How had he, several beds distant, sensed his oblate's wakefulness? Feeling not so much watched over as watched, Cormac shook his head, then whispered, "No, Brother Bernard. Naught."

"Then sleep."

"Yes. I'll try."

When the monk left his side, Cormac lay back, thinking how always when night came he and his brothers had fallen into sleep like stones. Yet here he was, the hours passing, unable even to keep his eyes closed.

In the afternoon, at the edge of the cliffs, he had abandoned his attempt at prayer, except to pray that the gift would be given him, as it had sometimes in

110

the past. What would Brother Bernard say to an oblate willing and eager to be accepted, to be tonsured and take vows, who yet found it difficult to pray?

Easy enough to know the answer.

Therefore, Cormac said to himself, he's not to know. Only to Prior Aelric, his confessor, would he confide this strange inability, which he could not think a public fault, but a most inner, troubling privation.

Sitting back on his heels he'd gazed out to sea, watching the seals, following the course of a curragh that appeared from the south. Two fishermen rowed in a circle, spreading a great cod net.

Yesterday, on that same sea, the Boyles and Brudairs had spread theirs.

Yesterday!

Seabirds screamed from daring nest sites built in cracks, crevices, narrow ledges all down the cliffside. Once, long ago, Prior Aelric had told him how for centuries the monks of this abbey had taken eggs from the more accessible nests, robbing but one from each nest.

"The way there are so many thousands of them," the priest had said, "they'll be happy to share with us, God's creatures, too."

Cormac could name most of the birds ... taught by Hugh Boyle. Boyle was the one had a tender feeling for God's lower creatures, and often said they comported themselves in a higher manner than did His higher creature, man himself. Kerry and Cormac thought he said it to goad their own da, who never failed of rising to Boyle's bait.

"Blasphemer!" Liam would roar. "You're after saying that man is not God's treasure, His first, beloved creation? He made the beasts of the field and the birds of the air for our use, did He not?"

"Not that I know," Boyle would reply, grinning. "Maybe He intended us to be for their use, but we being so sly turned the tables. Who can say?"

"*I* can say! If the beasts were meant to be above us, they'd be there. Can they speak? Can they sow or reap? Can they reason or pray?"

"For all that, they survive . . . and without killing their own kind, or murdering for sport. They do not build jails or dungeons to keep their fellows in. They do not claim merit and precedence according to how many possessions they've contrived to amass. No, no, Brudair—the more you argue with me, the more I think I'm in the right of it. Any beast is a man's better."

With Hugh Boyle, when he was arguing, it was often not possible to know how much to believe, but when he offered facts a person was on sure ground to trust him. So Cormac was able to name puffins and kittiwakes, murres and guillemots, petrels and shearwaters, nesting in their thousands on the steep cliffside, flinging themselves on air with the nonchalance of angels, stooping seaward to fish for their always famished young.

It pleased him, to be able to tell one from the other.

A bell had sounded from the church tower. It was calling the brothers to Sext, Cormac knew. He got to his feet and started back, hoping to find Brother Bernard. If not, he'd be too shy to go into the refectory by himself.

He need not have feared. Brother Bernard was obliged, from time to time, to confess in chapter and accept chastisement for a public backsliding. Usually short temper. But never did he shirk a duty, and he was waiting at the gate for Cormac, to take him in to dinner.

Now, lying in bed, Cormac thought that this was the longest day he had known in his fifteen years. And he thought, too, that here there would be no way to say that a day was in fact ended, since office followed office in daylight or dark.

After Compline, and a short time to walk in the cloister and exchange words with the others, if opportunity offered, which for Cormac it had not, all but the sacrist whose duty it was to prepare the church for Matins had retired.

Like the others, Cormac had divested himself of the brown habit he'd been given, hanging it on a peg above his bed. Then he lay down in his hose and shift to wait, wakeful and awed, for the ringing of the dorter bell that would signify Matins and Lauds.

Again the branch stirred at the window above him. Never before had he been in a room with a window. He had counted, wonderstruck, those in the dorter. Ten on each side, there were. High in the wall, and narrow.

Glancing toward Owen, who lay unmoving, Cormac

got stealthily to his feet, stood on the cot, and stretched till his eyes were even with the sill. For a long time he remained, looking through leaves, out at the night where clouds streaked across the white-faced moon. He could hear the surf, advancing, receding.

How believe he was here?

Lifting his eyes, he whispered, "Thank you, Lord."

The words fell from his lips like pebbles. True prayer rose—it did not fall.

Drawing a shaken breath, he let himself down, drew the blanket to his chin, and lay still. He waited, prayerless, for the bell.

When it came—a small, clear summons unlike the deep tone of the tower bell—he watched what Owen did, then pulled the habit over his head, and sat, sandaled, cowled, hands clasped in an attempt at silent prayer, waiting.

He was startled by a whisper from the next cot. "The office can last up to two hours, but do not fall asleep. Brother Bernard can hear an eyelid close. In the dark."

"Thank you," he whispered back. "I shan't fall asleep, but thank you—Owen."

Brother Bernard came down the row of beds, horn lamp held high. As he passed, each brother rose and followed, hands in sleeves, head bowed.

Down the stone night stairs the procession went, into the church where six candles were alight on the altar, though the monstrance remained hidden, only to appear at Mass.

At this, his first celebration of a holy office, in this community of the brothers among whom he hoped to spend the remainder of his life, Cormac leaned his lips on joined hands.

Now he could pray.

PART TWO
Ireland, A.D. 831

CHAPTER XII

T THE EDGE of the cliffs, Brother Cormac reclined on a bed of sea pinks. He shaded his eyes and tried to spy a lapwing whose song fell out of the clouds—"In beads of melody..."

He said this to himself, rejected it. He wished to keep his writing, and his thoughts, simple. *Beads of melody* was tempting, but overelaborate. Embellishment, richness, was for the illumination of books, not for the words.

And the lapwing was too high, too near Heaven's gate for a humble monk's sight.

Maher, Father Abbot, said that birds sang for the glory of God. Cormac did not doubt it. He thought, too, that they sang for joy, as Hugh Boyle had said long ago. As he himself, though not a choir monk, sang at Vespers to the glory of God surely, but also with the simple joy of lifting his voice freely, when most of life was passed in silence.

The tower bell was ringing for Sext, and still he lay, hands beneath his head, trying to empty his mind of thought, as bidden by his abbot. Just after Prime, Maher had come to the carrel in the scriptorium, where Cormac was bent over his work. He had, as usual, omitted the small refreshment of mixtum.

"Go for a walk," Abbot Maher had said. "Sit alone and do not think. Of anything. Go and simply *be*, under God's sky. You think too much. You overdo. You weary yourself."

"Oh, no, Father Abbot," Cormac replied, eyes on the manuscript upon which he had been at work for nigh on three years. "No. I never weary of this." He had glanced up mischievously, seizing this chance to speak aloud. "Working on the wall tires me. Scrubbing floors exhausts me...."

Maher lifted his eyes and sighed, but Cormac continued, smiling. "The mere thought of going down to the glen to help with the hay harvest leaves me stricken, makes me *sneeze*—"

"When the time comes, and as usual you anticipate your discomfort by several months, Brother Cormac, but when the time for harvest arrives you will go down with your scythe to sweat and labor with your fellows."

"Well do I know it, Father. I was not after looking for excuses, just making mention of how haying is labor and *this* is joy." He'd put a gentle hand on his book, his own book, his creation. Not a copy of some

120

other manuscript done to increase the volumes in their library for the greater learning of the community, but a book of his own making. His *Life of Saint Patrick.*

"Nonetheless," said the abbot. "Leave it awhile. Walk. Breathe an air innocent of ink and parchment. You look unmuscled, like a retired mule. And you are talking overmuch. Go."

Followed by Pangur Ban, he had come here to the cliff's edge, as they two had done times past reckoning in these past seventeen years. Here he would lie and dream, squinting at clouds, ignoring the gestures of brothers working on the wall who wished him to come and do his part. Just so, as a boy painting pictures on bark with the ink of berries and buttercups and moss, he had disregarded his father's summons bellowing through the woods.

"You do not make yourself loved, the way you keep apart from the rest of us," Owen had said again this morning, as he'd begun saying long ago, when they two had become professed monks, had taken their vows and received the cowl, had had their heads shaven in the tonsure, a monk's emblem of Christ's crown of thorns.

By then it had been plain to all that Cormac was different from the others. When still a novice, studying in his psalter under the exacting—in time cautiously laudatory—aegis of Brother Bernard, Cormac had proved a brand alight for learning.

He'd been barely tonsured when Brother Philip,

senior scribe, had given him permission to complete the missal left unfinished at the death of Joseph.

Now master of Latin, Irish, and Greek, he was the sole illuminator in the scriptorium. Brother Philip judged neither himself nor the two other scribes—young Kevin Tyrone, son of Tyrone, the High Chief, and Mark, a soldier's sprout who'd turned in horror from his father's life—equal to the inspiration that Cormac, mere yeoman's son, brought to his art.

Over the years, Philip, Kevin, Mark, and some scribes now dead, had recorded ancient classic lore, and holy scripture, psalms, and prayers to the glory of God. Manuscripts were borrowed, to copy, from other abbeys, as they lent their own, and the monastery library was grown to richness. It was glorious labor that, for Cormac, did not allow for cloister strolls or gossip at mixtum.

It earned him, from time to time, the familiar rebuke from Owen, a brother who did not scorn to repeat himself. "To keep apart from parlor, from mixtum," he had said last night, as they prepared for sleep, cots still side by side, "scarcely availing yourself of the opportunity to speak. Can you not understand how it makes the rest of us feel—uncomfortable. Callow."

"Owen—I would not for any measure make anyone feel in any way uncomfortable. As to callow—wouldn't you say that some of our brethren merit the description?"

"I'd say your saying that is a fault of which I could well accuse you in chapter. Criticizing."

"Commenting, actually."

"You really do feel superior to the rest of us, Cormac, do you not?"

"Not. I just want to be getting on with my work. If that makes me appear to feel superior—it's a burden I must bear. This life is brief, my book will be a long time in the making, and I am obliged to make a choice, apparently—to be loved, as you put it, or to finish my history of Saint Patrick. No—I do *not* make the choice. It has been made for me."

"By God, I suppose," Owen had snapped.

Cormac was imperturbable. "Possibly," he'd replied, pulling the blanket to his chin.

He knew well what irritated Owen, infirmarer since Brother Francis, God rest him, had been laid in the monks' burial ground. The same emotion that had caused others in the past to accuse him, in chapter, of sloth. They still considered him a shirker, some saying it to his face, they looking puzzled as they spoke. Because, where work in the scriptorium was concerned, all knew he was tireless. He labored, insisting it was not to be called that, all the daylight hours when not called to Mass or the daily offices. He did not linger over meals in the refectory, or appear at mixtum or idle in the cloister after Vespers.

He knew he was resented, and admired, possibly envied, and thought this strange indeed. But not the resentment, admiration or envy of his brothers troubled him.

What caused him daily—hourly—pain was that he could not yet feel a devotion to God that was greater than his love of books.

123

He prayed.

He implored Heaven to grant him grace to find exaltation in the endless laying of stones upon the abbey walls that seemed, like the walls of his boyhood, always in need of repair. He wanted to sing as he toiled at the knee-bruising task of scrubbing the cold stone slabs of the church floor, to whistle while engaged in the sweaty, fly-plagued threshing and binding of hay, or in the turning of the quern to grind corn. His father, long ago, had offered to grind the monks' corn at his mill, but Abbot Maher declined, explaining that toil was good for his flock.

Cormac had no doubt that it was. He still hoped for the day when toil would find him singing.

His father. When had he last thought of his father? Of any of those, some dear, with whom he had lived for the first part of his life? Fifteen when he came here. Thirty-two now.

He could go weeks, months, without calling his family to mind. It was not for lack of love—or anyway, love of Kerry and his mother—that he forgot them. It was the monastic life that brought forgetfulness.

Except for festal days, the routine of the abbey flowed from office to office, chapter to chapter, mass to mass, season to season in so steady a course that in time a man scarcely knew if he was living yesterday or tomorrow.

He had last seen his brother Kerry at Christmas. They had met in the parlor, Cormac given dispensation to speak freely, and as in Christmases past, had tried to crowd into sixty minutes all they had thought to say to each other in the year gone by.

At each Christmas meeting, since first he'd come here, there had seemed to be the same news of crops and flocks, of death. Always news of death. Mag and Bos, replaced. A farm could not be without a dog, an ox. A few years ago Kerry had said proudly that they now had a mule besides.

Gammer had outlived her son and her son's wife, and then on a spring night quietly followed after them.

"Do you remember how she used to tell us stories at night, before Mither took over?" Cormac had asked, but Kerry did not.

"I see only the shadow of an old woman in a corner," he confessed.

Some years ago—eight, was it?—Kerry had told how he and Natt had fallen disastrously in love with the same girl. Eileen Boyle. "Ah, she's the lass with the delicate air," said Kerry, shaken with emotion. "I shall *die* if I don't win her. That Natt—" He'd curled his lip. "He's grown to a great brute of a fellow that could wrestle an oak to the ground, and not one thought more in his head than when you last laid eyes on him."

"I don't recall that he had a thought, unless Dal gave it him," Cormac had said, not unkindly, just speaking truth.

It was Kerry won and wed Eileen, and Natt, not Dal, who went for a soldier. "An archer up at the castle," Kerry said. "With his very own arrow slit in the merlon to aim through. He took me up to show it off. God,

Cor—that castle is the bleakest, coldest, dankest place ever you did see. I'd not trade the cottage Eileen and I share for ten such bastions. Oh, but if you could see Natt, helmet and buckler and such an air on him as would make you roar with laughter." He'd given Cormac a sideways glance. "That is, if yer allowed to laugh at all within these walls?"

"Once a month," Cormac said soberly. "By special permission of the abbot."

"Oh, now, Cor—I didn't mean to scoff."

"Of course not," the monk had said, smiling.

"You know, the longer I live," Kerry said once, and only the once, "the longer I live and know love, and a child coming along now that it makes me heart ache to think of, already I love him so—the longer I live, Cor, the less I understand how you can live like this— immured here. Do you find yerself missing us? Missing, anyway, the *world*?"

Cormac had put a hand on this best-loved brother's arm and said, "I do not miss the 'world,' or even you. I think of you, and long for this visit. I love you. But here I belong, and no other place. You can't understand, I can't explain. Let it be, Kerry. We've found our places, you and I. Tell me how you and Dal manage together, now that you have the farm between you?"

"We disagree still on everything that matters, *except* for how the farm should go. There we pull in double yoke without upsetting the cart. I think, Cor, that each feels enormous contempt for the other. It makes for a peculiar kind of peace, since we manage to work together with hardly a word spoken."

They had parted, he and his brother, this past Christmas as on Christmases before, fondly, with little pain. The ache of separation was not for the men they'd become, but for the boys they had been, and boyhood was long past.

Cormac had awakened refreshed from a short sleep, to find Pangur Ban humming on his chest. Is there, he wondered, another sound in nature so untroubled and undemanding, so demurely self-applauding as a cat's purr?

"Sometimes," he said, "I think I would not mind changing places with you, little brother. Except that you cannot read," he added. Old, old was Pangur Ban. As was Abbot Maher. Both tranquil in their great age. . . . Pangur unaware of approaching death. Maher preparing a welcome.

As a boy, Cormac had been unable to guess the abbot's age, only thinking he was an old man. And so he had been, even then. Now he was ancient, a little stooped, growing forgetful, but still with his firm mien and gentle air of authority, his way of making decisions not always according to the Rule.

God's man, but also his own, Abbot Maher.

Putting Pangur aside, Cormac got to his feet and looked toward the east, where lay miles of farm enclosures, of forest, of pastures where sheep and cattle grazed or lay ruminating. He could see the very field where he and Kerry and Mag had watched their flock by night, under skies full of nesting stars.

He could descry the castle, a stony bastion on a hill lower than this cliff to which the monastery clung. Still, an eminence in the glen. Where in all that guarded and bristling fortification was his brother, Natt, so proud of his buckler and bow, his very own slit in the merlon? Dal and Kerry on the farm. Liam and Megeen and Gammer—God rest them—dead. Meg married. Day followed day, month month, year year—and what no child could believe or predict had happened to him and his brothers, as it did to all children. Their seemingly immortal parents had proved mortal, and they themselves were grown and growing toward the grave.

So be it, thought Brother Cormac. He looked for a moment longer across the glen, at the sky where hung an afternoon moon, white as a turnip.

He turned to face the sea, and drew a sharp whistling breath.

Lifting over the horizon, at the distant rim of the sea, looking as his mother had described them in the cottage long ago, were the striped sails of the Northmen.

As she had feared, Gammer predicted, and neither lived to see, the Vikings were coming again to Ireland. . . .

CHAPTER XIII

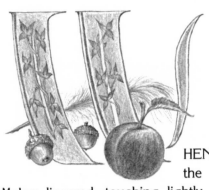

HEN CORMAC HAD left the scriptorium, Abbot Maher lingered, touching lightly with one finger the vellum sheet upon which this Heaven-gifted monk was at work...a page from his history of Saint Patrick.

For several years now, Brother Cormac had done only the illuminations in a growing collection of holy and classical literature that was the chief treasure of the abbey.

Skilled copyists wrote the texts, in Latin, Irish, sometimes in Greek, and eye-aching, finger-cramping labor it was, at which none complained.

Well, Maher amended indulgently, complained little.

From time to time a scribe, toilworn and quite possibly bored after months of copying, in minuscule or majuscule, words from which perhaps meaning had departed, would put a wholly personal postscript on the most sacred of volumes. Once—Maher smiled—a young brother had penned the words, *Thank God, thank God, and again oh again, thank God, I have reached the end of this missal!* His cursive had been as exquisite in this final outcry as in the thousands of lines that went before.

With his history of Saint Patrick, however, Cormac was doing all. He had cured and scraped and stoned and bleached the lambskin sheets to folios of pale satiny smoothness. That alone had taken months. Then, leaving spaces for the illuminated capitals, he had written the story of the great fifth-century saint, equaled in honor in Ireland only by Saint Columba.

Making almost a romance of it, Cormac recounted how Patrick, the young Roman Briton, had been taken in slavery by Irish pirates and put to tending swine in the hills. How his loneliness had been blessed by an angelic visit, in which he was told to escape and acquire learning and become an ordained priest. And how after many years, he had heard in a vision the voice of this pagan island beseeching him to return and walk amongst them, preaching the Word.

So Patrick had established his church on the hill now called Croagh Patrick, bringing the Faith to Ireland in a bloodless conversion. Cormac had made much of that, telling Maher that he had encountered in his reading more slain martyrs than he could erase from his mind. Their blood, the abbot knew, troubled the sleep of this inspired, wool-gathering monk whose indolent body contained a mind that coursed like a hare. Cormac brooded equally over God's martyrs and His creatures that had no protection against man.

He would have no blood in this book.

So here were the many pages, written in carbon ink and ink from the squeezed gall of acorns and peaches, wearing out who knew how many swan's-quill pens. The text was complete, and Cormac now at the work that he loved—the illumination.

Stopping only for daily offices, for plain refectory meals that seemed to mean little to him beyond necessary nourishment, performing what manual labor he could in no way escape—it could not be denied that he did what he could to dodge his share—Cormac was spending his life in the scriptorium.

Could this, the abbot asked himself, asked Prior Aelric, asked Bernard, be the right path? Was Cormac living the Rule? Surely he and Aelric and Bernard were guilty of lax interpretation where this one brother was concerned? They had allowed him to assume the tonsure and the cowl when unsure of his vocation, questioning whether his devotion to God was entire.

They were unsure yet.

"He is an artist," Maher murmured, turning as Bernard entered the room. "Ah, Bernard," he said, vexed at being caught talking to himself, "I've been meaning to ask whether the new oblate, Stephen, is—"

He broke off, glancing again at the folio of Saint Patrick. "How beautiful this is, Bernard. How almost heartbreakingly beautiful."

Bernard nodded.

"Do you not think it possible that we have in our

131

midst a great"—the abbot paused, chose a humbler word—"a *fine* artist?"

Bernard studied the page before them, and abandoned discretion. "Possibly a great one, Father. One of those touched, *ab ovo*, by the finger of God."

"Then who are we, Bernard, you or I or Aelric, to judge or to direct? No, I do not regret our decision to accept him in the cloister, nor can I think us wrong to give him his head—even though the others grumble. But I pray that one day he will put his joy in writing and painting second to his exultation in serving God."

"Amen," said Brother Bernard.

The two old men looked at each other a moment longer. As the abbot continued silent, Bernard departed.

Abbot Maher watched him go, thinking there had been something he'd intended to ask the novice master. Say to him? This mislaying of thoughts happened to him with a regularity that made him uneasy. He would form an idea, begin a bidding to one of the community, and in the flick of a lash find his mind blank of recollection.

Only this morning he had started toward the wall with clear notion of consulting Brother Terence as to—as to what? Cudgel his brain as he would, there remained no trace of what he had been planning to say to—ask of?—Brother Terence. Had it been important? Something that should not be left undone? Or a simple notion as well lost as voiced?

If I do not know, thought the old abbot, perhaps harm will come of my forgetfulness?

132

"Am I, Lord, too ancient for the burden I have happily carried these many years?" he asked.

He could leave the abbey, leave it in younger, firmer hands. Prior Aelric's hands. He could go into the far hills, become an anchorite, a hermit. He would be alone then, with God, and with God's creatures that gave him pleasure as they did Cormac.

He had spent his life in the silent, worshiping, working company of brothers. Surely now, without guilt, he could be alone.

To end life in the company of the high-hinded hare, the nimble-footed vixen, the clattering hedgehog—a hermit in its own spiney right—could he ask more? Oh, then he could listen in peace, without responsibility, to the belling of the stag, the songlike chorus of wolf packs. To the aubades of birds, feathered bards that sang to God but also—Cormac was in the right of it—for their own lyric joy.

He had been a poet once, before taking the cowl.

None knew it here, but he had been a bard celebrated in the court of a High King.

He took a deep breath, recalling castles and feasting, harping and richly gowned courtiers, himself in fur and silk like the rest. Saint Benedict had said, "Wear not the furs of beasts, nor the work of worms." But he had not known that then, and he singing of Irish heroes slain in battle while all the court listened and applauded.

He remembered, too, a glen in the Wicklow hills where that king's domain had stretched for miles. One

133

day he had taken a horse and ridden out alone in the forest of ancient oaks. It was there, in that branchy church, that he concluded to leave the world of men and find sanctuary in an abbey, where he could live for God.

Now here he was, an old man beginning to be forgetful, but could still recall that glen, and the quiet there, and the vow he had made, and kept, and never regretted. A man could go back to such a place and wait for God's finger to beckon him Home. In that nature-solaced solitude, what he remembered or what forgot would be of no more moment than whether an oak leaf fell from the tree in the morning or the evening.

It was a wonderfully tranquil vision.

Ah—he reaped the random question concerning the new oblate, Stephen, that had been interrupted by his and Bernard's study of Cormac's manuscript. It no longer seemed important. Was, in any case, Bernard's problem.

Examining his hands to be sure they were quite clean, he picked up the top leaf in cautious fingers, holding it close to his dim-sighted eyes.

It was a carpet page, an entire sheet without words—like a tapestry. In brilliant color, in blues, greens, and reds, Cormac presented the saint seated on a throne touched with gold.

They had obtained the rare, fragile, infinitesimally thin, infinitely precious sheets of gold leaf from the abbey at Rosserk, in exchange for an entire gospel.

Cormac had surrounded Saint Patrick with six-winged angels, and birds, and little beasts. Here—the abbot squinted—here at the blessed feet were a nursing sow, to represent the years that Saint Patrick had tended swine. Toying with the hem of the saint's gown was a white cat.

Pangur Ban, of course. A creature as old in feline years, the abbot mused, as I in human ones.

Cormac's companion, friend. Confidant? Even that was possible.

In the upper right corner of the carpet page was a waterwheel, and—holding the page away now, hoping perhaps to see better that way—the abbot made out the forms of two otters riding a cataract into a pond. What a fancy!

At the bottom left corner was a cow with calf nursing.

Everywhere, peering through vines and yellow gorse and flowering shrubs, were little foxes, tiny field mice, rabbits....

Abbot Maher put the sheet back on the desk, closed his eyes.

Such fatigue would never alter now, when to gaze upon a work so stirring as this blurred his vision, when merely to hold it to his eyes made his arms ache intolerably.

He turned away, turned back.

In taking up the carpet page, he had uncovered another, quite unlike the closely written minuscule sheets of the saint's history. This seemed to be— appeared to be—a poem.

135

Drawing a stool close to the desk, the abbot leaned over to fix his nearsighted eyes on a page of which the capital letter was a great *I*. Trailing down the left-hand margin was a blossoming vine, woven upon a trellis, adorned with elaborate embellishments and gilt interlacings upon which insects and birds seemed actually to flutter.

"Ah, Cormac," murmured the abbot. "Can you not stay with your day's work, even when your day's work is your delight? What has this poem to do with your history? What has a cat, any cat, to do with the Saint of Ireland?"

He read.

> *I and Pangur Ban my cat,*
> *'Tis a like task we are at:*
> *Hunting mice is his delight,*
> *Hunting words I sit all night.*
>
> *'Tis a merry thing to see*
> *At our tasks how glad are we*
> *When at home we sit and find*
> *Entertainment to our mind.*
>
> *'Gainst the wall he sets his eye*
> *Full and fierce and sharp and sly:*
> *'Gainst the wall of knowledge I*
> *All my little wisdom try.*
>
> *So in peace our task we ply,*
> *Pangur Ban, my cat and I:*
> *In our arts we find our bliss,*
> *I have mine and he has his.*

Twined amongst the flowers, the leaves, the vines and nesting birds, the butterflies, Cormac had been so bold as to ink in small—nonetheless quite visible—letters, *Cormac me fecit.*

"Cormac made me" the abbot said softly, aloud. And to himself, "He has too much of pride. He will always be Art's first, and God's second. But if I can understand, so surely will God."

He rose stiffly, put the carpet page back upon the poem, and turned to leave the scriptorium as Cormac and Prior Aelric entered, faces drained of color, eyes wide with portent.

What had brought looks of such ill omen to ordinarily placid, monkish features? Something dire, something terrible and—Maher knew—already irreversible.

"What is it, Aelric?" he asked calmly. "Tell what you have to tell."

Cormac knelt. "Father Abbot—far out on the horizon, miles away yet, but approaching, are the longboats of the Vikings."

CHAPTER XIV

OR A MOMENT, Abbot Maher seemed to totter, then straightened from what had become a customary stoop. Describing a cross in air, he said, *"In omnia paratus."*

At all times ready? Cormac thought. Not for this. They were not, could not be, ready for this.

"Aelric," said the abbot, "have Terence ring the bell. Call everyone to chapter. There is much to be done. How far, Cormac, do you think they are from landing?"

"Hours yet, Father Abbot."

"I see. Aelric, send novices down to the glen. They will ask the nearest farmers to bring wagons, so that we can take away the monastery treasures. That would be your father, and Hugh Boyle, Cormac. They will come at our bidding—"

138

Cormac did not point out what the abbot had forgot—that his own father was dead. Hugh Boyle would come as fast as his mule would pull the cart. And Dal and Kerry, too. And others close by, though few close by enough.

"The Ui Niall and I have had an understanding," the abbot went on, "through all these years during which the Northmen have left us in peace, that should—or rather when—they came again, the library and altar treasures would be stored in the souterrain of the castle. Probably these sacking savages will root them out, but we must make an effort to preserve what we can. Especially the books."

When the community was assembled in parlor, Abbot Maher addressed them in a voice strengthened by peril.

"My children, you know now that the Vikings are approaching our shores, and for what purpose. We have been spared for many years the horror of their raids, and for those years, let us give thanks. What remains is to flee. We will carry down the cliffside all our books, and our few but precious altarpieces, to a place of greater safety—"

Few indeed, thought Cormac. Theirs was a leanly furnished church, and a spare altar. A gold-and-silver monstrance, gift of the Ui Niall. Two filigree silver candlesticks, gift of the O'Hara. A gem-studded reliquary, said by all and believed by some to contain a lock of hair from the head of Saint Cirian, and a paring from his fingernail. That from the Tyrone. There was a linen altar cloth, fine as silk, that the noble ladies of the castle had embroidered and given to the abbey. Rich gifts in exchange for the monks' prayers from people too worldly occupied to spend much time in prayer themselves.

"When we have taken, in the farmers' carts, everything we can carry," said Maher, "and hidden it deep in the castle souterrain, which the High Chief says he will then block up with boulders, we shall ourselves seek what asylum from the vandals is possible. The Ui Niall and I think that the greatest safety—I fear it will not be great—lies in the fortification of the castle. But if any of you wish instead to be with your families and face this danger at their side, go with my blessing."

He glanced toward the door. "Yes, Brother Owen?"

"The wagons are at the foot of the cliff, Father Abbot."

Abbot Maher closed his eyes. "My children—let us pray," he said in a firm voice. "Deliver us, oh Lord, from this peril if it should be thy will, but let us face all danger in calm and Christian faith in thine infinite wisdom." He clasped his palms to his lips, and the community bowed its head.

"And now, to work. Prior Aelric will direct. Take the books first. Carefully, carefully—but I need not say that."

He moved his right hand in air, again describing the cross. "Go now, with my blessing."

Cormac went, not to the library, but to the scriptorium, making no excuse to himself for what he was about to do. As nothing could alter his intention, why attempt to justify it?

Outside, the work of removal went on. Usually, when working anywhere about the abbey, the monks kilted their habits and tossed back their cowls for easier motion. Now they moved down the steep steps cut in the rock face of the cliff in silent procession, fully garbed and hooded, as if to meet these ravaging Danes in holy armor.

As the others streamed from church and library, carrying the precious, the invaluable if few treasures of the abbey, Brother Cormac, at his desk in the scriptorium, took a large piece of cowhide, a length of leather lacing, and an awl. Driving holes through the hide, he laid his history of Saint Patrick in the center. His grief was keen that he had not had time to complete it, yet he could not spare time to grieve. He folded the hide several times before beginning to sew.

On the desk beside him, Pangur Ban sat watching. No purring now. Cormac wondered if in his small bright brain he was aware of an alteration in the air. Unable in any way to meet or resist it, did this cat, his friend, in some fashion recognize peril?

No, thought Cormac, steadily sewing, but watching too as the gold eyes closed, and the old head drooped till the cat slept, nose in his paws. No—like his fellow creatures, there is only the moment, the present, for Pangur.

A shadow fell athwart him, and he went on sewing.

"Brother Cormac. Look at me."

Getting to his feet, then to his knees, Cormac

looked up at his abbot. "I cannot—I do not—the souterrain will not—" He stopped, sighed, went on. "I hope, I trust to God, Father Abbot, that our holy treasures will be safe in the castle—"

"But you do not trust Him to safeguard your book."

"Oh, Father—give me leave to protect it in my own way. It is my life. I would give my life in exchange for it. Let me put it where I think it—where even if it is not safer than in the souterrain it will be no less so. And when this is over, I will know where to find it. If—" He broke off, one fist to his mouth.

"If you are alive to find it."

"Yes."

"You have never been master of your pride, Cormac. I think you do not try to subdue it."

"It is not *self*-pride, Father. Not fondness for myself. It is for my book. Only that. Always that," he ended helplessly.

"Which book *is* yourself."

Cormac, still kneeling, did not reply.

"Ah, my dear son," said the old man, sitting on one of the scribes' low stools. "What can I say now? You may be asking a deathbed boon of me. Can I deny it? Have you—" It almost seemed that he would laugh. "Have you the intention of assisting the others, who are after trudging up and down the long cliff steps with the—the rest of what is valuable here? I think there is not much time to waste, and every hand is needed. Will you evade even this last task that may be asked of you?"

142

"After I am finished here. Then I shall—"

"Cormac!" The abbot gestured with one hand. "Get up, get up. You cannot complete your sewing properly whilst you kneel there. To the very end, you shirk your share of the labor, but I am not so foolish as to insist now."

"Is it the very end, then, Father?" Cormac took up the awl and resumed sewing. "It—they—are they quite as bad as my mother told us long ago?"

The abbot braced himself against the desk, straightened, and said, "I have known these savages twice before. They have nothing in them of pity or ruth, no way of comprehending a pain not their own. They will savage the countryside, killing for sport. What they cannot take with them, they will burn—barns, farms, fields. This abbey. Once, about eighty years ago, it was sacked and laid waste by these pirates. But we rebuilt, always we shall rebuild. If not we, those who follow us."

He shook his head and clasped his arms together, rocking from side to side. "They take slaves, in irons. There is no horror of which they are incapable, and no prayer or plea can reach them. So then, yes. I think it is the end. Unless the Ui Niall and his warriors can hold out."

Now Natt will have cause to do more than admire his bow, thought Cormac, and said, "You don't believe they can hold out."

"I think that the Irish are redoubtable, and in a strange way—one we cannot fathom—even gallant in their border skirmishes. I do not believe that they are able to understand how to meet the Northmen. Nor withstand them."

"I see."

There was silence while Cormac completed the job of encasing his book as tightly as possible. Then, removing the contents of a large banded tin box— unused parchment sheets that it pained him to leave here—he wedged his package within.

"What will you do now?" the abbot asked in a voice grown passive.

"Take it to a place I know of. What are you going to do?"

"Wait."

"Wait? For what? Where?"

"Here. For whatever comes."

Cormac leaped to his feet. "Do not say so! You are going to go down the cliffside and be taken in one of the wagons to the castle, where you'll be safe. Safer. You may not wait here. I will not allow you to—"

"I have sent Aelric and the wagons on their way. The treasures must be got to safety. The wagons are full, the brothers and Aelric have to walk beside them, and the time is short."

"Do you mean that Aelric *agreed* to leave you here?"

"Prior Aelric, Cormac. Although you have never seemed to understand this—the Rule is explicit. The abbot is to be obeyed. Aelric protested, but submitted. I am his abbot, he must do as I say. Everyone in the community must do as I say. Except you."

There was enormous fatigue in his voice, but no reproach. "I could not climb down the cliffside in any case. Or walk to the castle."

"You could ride in a wagon. Room must be made for you. I'll run and catch them up, the way they'll stay for you, and I'll *carry* you down the cliff—"

"No. I have done what I think best, and there's an end on it."

Cormac pressed a hand on the old priest's shoulder. "Come with me, then. I can easily carry you."

The abbot glanced at the desk. "Me, and that great tin box, besides? And—Pangur Ban? You'll not be leaving him behind?"

"Of course not." Cormac sighed hugely, bit his lip, stared around the bare scriptorium. He sank again to his knees.

"Father Abbot, I am a swift runner—"

Maher smiled.

"Nonetheless—I am, when needs must. I shall take my book to a place I know of, not far from this, where I hope it will be safe. It may be it will be protected by the hedgehog and the hare and even the wolf. The wolves will come closer now, with the people of the glen in retreat behind the castle walls."

"Strange guardians you look for."

"As good, perhaps, as the Ui Niall's archers. Is there any sure safety now?"

"No."

"The longboats are still some distance offshore. I have time to hide my book."

"Still you say *my*."

145

"Forgive me, Father, my arrogance. Give me a penance—then. I merit one."

The abbot held up a quelling hand. "Of course the book is yours. It is what you came here to create, and I have no doubt that God will take that into account when you try to tell *Him* that you had the call. And don't trouble me about penances at this time. If you are penitent—I say, *if*—God will know that, too."

"But—"

"No. He sees all. And Prior Aelric and I saw much. We made our decision and do not regret it." He tipped his head back, closing his eyes. "You had best go now, Cormac."

"I will be back. Soon. Stay here with Pangur Ban. Wait for me, and I will carry you and him the way to the castle, where we'll be safe."

"God willing."

"God willing. Your blessing, Father."

"My blessing, always, Cormac, my very dear son."

Brother Cormac picked up his box and ran, taking the cliff steps recklessly. Along the boreen he raced, down the path leading to his brothers' farm, empty now of habitation. He looked with grave sadness at the sheep, at the cow whose name he did not know, peacefully grazing in their pasture. Living, like Pangur, in the moment. What would be their future? He hoped the Vikings would find them worthy of capture, not slaughter.

He sped up the cowlane, past the mill, into the woods to the badger set where he trusted that even should no human eye look upon it again, his book would lie here safe, through the years to come.

Yet he let himself hope that one day, too far in the future for calculation, when the world had grown peaceful—and surely such a time must come—his book would be found, and tenderly dealt with. Even cherished.

Pulling his old paint board from the deep hole, his rook quills and broken saucer, he spared a moment to be thankful that they were still here, undisturbed. Even if the Northmen should scour the woods for prisoners, why notice a disused badger set lying well off the lane? The filched cowhide that had caused his father such vexation long ago was in here still.

He wrapped the box within it for further protection, and thrust this work of his life deep within the tunnel. Blocking the entrance with stones, he draped strands of ivy to grow across it.

He knelt and prayed aloud.

"Lord dear, if it should so please You, let this book lie safe. Let not the Vikings find it. And Lord, if I am overproud, believe that I am wretched and grieved for it. I could not do otherwise. You, Who know all, know that."

With a final look at this place where he had been so content as a boy, he crossed himself and started back to the abbey, to his abbot, and his cat.

The Vikings came ashore.

PART THREE
England and Ireland, A.D. 1169

CHAPTER XV

T WAS SEVERAL hours yet before Prime. In Cerne Abbey, near Weymouth, the dormitories, the guesthouse, the infirmary lay under the spell of sleep. Not a uniformly silent sleep. Here and there a novice stirred and murmured, a troubled guest turned and sighed, a sick man cried.

The great gates were closed and locked, the only entrance now through the wicket, where pitch torches flared at the porter's lodge. The light of them leaped and shuddered on the ice-sheeted road that led past the monastery. Built by the Romans centuries before, it still served.

Within the lodge, the porter nodded, half asleep. Through his doze he could hear the bark of a hunting owl, the far-off chorus of a wolf pack, the creaking of wintry boughs. Once hoofbeats neared the gate with a ringing clatter and the porter, instantly awake, ran out to the wicket.

The rider went on by. Why abroad so late, on so bitter chill a night, the porter wondered, shivering. He glanced upward. A moonless sky, encrusted with stars. Bits of ice, were they, as some said? He looked across the dark cloister to the abbot's quarters. Still alight. Why? Well, he'd never know. He hurried back to the lodge, where a small brazier made a lovely warmth.

In the abbot's parlor, lit by wall sconces, Abbot Brendan and his prior, Ruthven, were talking quietly. They sat close to the hearth where a fire failed to warm the chill of the room.

"You will understand, Father Abbot," Prior Ruthven was saying, "why I want now to be returning to my own country, I not having set foot upon her blessed earth in sixty years. Sixty-three."

"Of course, Ruthven. But will you not wait until the weather is milder? This is the coldest winter in my recollection," said the abbot, who was young.

"Or in mine," said the prior, who was old. Weather did not affect him. Or, rather, its effects did not affect him. He had chilblains, age had bruised his very bones, but he was indifferent to bodily discomfort.

He was dying, and intended, God willing, to die in Ireland.

"I have never asked before," the abbot said tentatively, "but perhaps you will forgive me if I do so now—why is that you chose to take the cowl in England, rather than in Ireland that you love so?"

The prior's wrinkled ancient face took on a look of mischief. "Ah, Brendan—will you truly have an answer, so?"

"I confess I am curious."

"Very well. I came here and made my vows and remained here most of my life, as an offering to God. Your climate is the most miserable I have ever known, and I've grown to accept it. Even by abbey standards, the food is wretched. I learned to eat for nourishment, not for pleasure. In Ireland, at Ballyvaghan, life would have been—easier. The air gentler. The food, even by abbey standards, tasty. Oh, do not mistake—the monks of Ballyvaghan lead lives as rigorous and dutiful as any in England, but in some way not their doing softer. It's the air of Ireland does it. We have hard winters there, but somehow not so—hostile. And spring comes to my country long before it comes to this. So, Brendan—I exiled myself, for God. Now I wish to go back, and doubt not He will understand."

"And you feel you cannot wait till spring?"

"I know I cannot." He looked affectionately at this brilliant young abbot. "All my life, Brendan, until these past months, my mind was a servant who came at my call, my body a mule that toiled as I did. I must get both back to Ireland before the mule collapses and the mind scarpers altogether."

"Very well, Ruthven, my dear old friend. But I will

153

not permit you to go alone. Such a trip even in summer would be harrowing." He poured a measure of abbey wine in two small crystal glasses, handed one to his prior, who took it thankfully. "One of the young brothers will go with you. See you safe to Ballyvaghan."

"Well. I won't say no to that. Mind, an intelligent one. I propose to die, Brendan, but not of boredom."

The abbot smiled. "What would you say to Brother Fergus?"

Ruthven's eyes brightened. "Oh, excellent. He's learned, and not too pious."

"You doubt his piety?" Abbot Brendan said quickly.

"I have no reason to. He does not wear it like larding on a roast, like some we have here. In truth, I am not well acquainted with him. But I like him. Comes of the gentry, does he not?"

"Minor, climbing gentry," said Abbot Brendan, who was of noble stock and had never, though he scourged himself for it, subdued a remnant of pride. "His father is a dandy and a buffoon. And, for all that, a hard, driving man, possessed by ambition. Possessed by possessions, of which he has many, not all honorably acquired. He holds it against us that Fergus chose the cowl over the court. This is not gossip, Ruthven. These are facts."

Gossip or fact, Ruthven was not interested, except to wonder under what compulsion Fergus had come to the abbey. "So—not with his father's blessing, was it, Brendan?"

"Far from it."

"Do you think he has a vocation?"

"I feel he has. It will take time to be sure. Men come to the cloister for many reasons."

Ruthven nodded. "One of the postulants said to me this morning that outside the wall he felt a worm in the terrors of the universe. Within, he feels safe."

"Oh, dear. Not good. Which one?"

"Mark."

"God willing, we can help him."

"It will take God's help, surely, besides our own."

They brooded in silence a moment before the abbot went on.

"A lad like Fergus, brought up with every material indulgence, would find our austerity repellent, had he not a spiritual calling. He certainly isn't a saint. God knows, Ruthven, we can't afford to fill the place with those. There'd be no work done." He smiled. "Still, I hope someone comes to replace you, our closest approach to the beatific."

The old monk frowned. "Even in fun, Father Abbot, you go too far."

"Perhaps not."

"Enough. This young brother who is to go with me. He's a scribe, is he not?"

"Yes. And hopes to become an illuminator. There's no doubt he will be, but I'll not permit him to rush his fences. He lacks patience, and must learn it."

"We've all had to learn that, so."

"Some are better students than others. Nonetheless, he's a good young man, and strong. I would feel secure, knowing you had him to rely upon."

155

"Then it's settled. I should like to start today, after Prime."

"So soon?"

"None too soon."

Shortly after dawn, the two monks, bundled in woolen winter habits and shawls, set off on mules for the port at Ilfracombe, there to take ship for the Irish coast.

"A pity," said Fergus, as the animals trudged along, "that the abbey didn't run to horses for us. They have a few fairly good mounts."

"I asked for mules, Fergus. I've ridden this old fellow, Brume, for years. When occasion for riding offered atall, which was not often. He'll stay with me when you start back on—what's that fellow's name?" he asked, glancing at the large mule beside him.

"Jackstraw. If he were a horse, he'd be mettlesome. He shows spirit, even for what he is."

"So long as he does not show it overmuch," said Ruthven, setting his jaw, resolved not to let this lively young monk know how, at the very start of their long journey, he was feeling fatigued. He had no doubt that Abbot Brendan had been after giving orders for their immediate return, should his old friend seem to be failing.

Not Brendan, not Fergus here, was part of his life now. He would reach Ballyvaghan either because of or despite them, but reach it he would.

They made Ilfracombe in good time, on a glorious

cold morning of westerly winds that would fill the sails to drive them swiftly toward Ireland. The sea was an expanse of little wavelets, tossing and glinting under a sky like a bowl of silk.

Gazing toward the far shore, Ruthven knew a sense of fathomless content.

"Fergus," he said, when they were aboard ship, sitting at the prow, "in the abbey at Ballyvaghan there is a reliquary containing, or said to contain, a lock of hair and a fingernail paring from Saint Cirian. To be sure, it is difficult to know when the Irish are speaking with absolute knowledge and when afloat upon a sea of fantasy—but it is there, the reliquary. I think you will be allowed to see it, perhaps even touch it."

Fergus stared, openmouthed. He hadn't dreamed, when informed that he was to accompany the old prior to his last resting place, that such a glorious possibility lay ahead. He had been glad enough of the trip. A chance to stretch not only his legs, but his spirits, a chance to ride for days (he'd thought then on a horse) in the bracing winter air, to cross the channel and travel clear across Ireland—all that had seemed gift enough.

But that there should be the reliquary of a saint at journey's end! He dismissed Ruthven's doubts. If he, Fergus, was to be so blessed as to see and touch a casket containing the relics of a saint, then that casket must contain what it was said to contain.

Never doubting his devotion to God, Fergus was equally untroubled by self-doubt.

157

Abbot Brendan had excused them, in the interests of hastening the trip, from daily offices, except for Compline and Prime. Each evening they stopped at some farm, some cottier's hut, asking shelter for the night, which was not refused them.

When the simple fare they carried in their saddle-bags was exhausted, they asked for a loaf, a bit of cheese, and water, refusing more if it was pressed upon them. Each evening, at Compline, Prior Ruthven took out his small traveling altar, placed upon it the chalice with the Host, and said Mass with the family under whose roof or in whose barn they found themselves.

There were times when Fergus feared for his prior, when the old man was obliged to dismount and lie on the cold ground before recovering strength to continue. Now too far along on the trip to turn back, Fergus feared that he might have to bring Ruthven into the abbey at Ballyvaghan not astride his mule but over it.

Once he said, "Prior Ruthven—if it should fall out that you—that you cannot— If it came about that—"

"If I should die on the way."

"Yes. What would we do about absolution? I am not a priest like you. Could you give yourself last rites? We can't have you die unshriven. Father Abbot would never forgive me."

Ruthven smiled at the young monk's priorities, but said only, "Of course I have thought of that, Fergus. And, of course, it is not possible for me to shrive myself. I believe a sincere act of contrition would serve. Still, I think you needn't trouble yourself on that score. I'll get to Ballyvaghan on my feet. That is to say, on Brume's."

For the most, it was a cheerful journey. Released from the customary vow of silence, and both of them good talkers, they grew as close, it seemed to Fergus, as father and son. Indeed, he felt close to this old monk as he never had to his own father, a hot-tempered squire of pretensions with his eye on a knighthood that he planned to buy if there was no way to earn it.

"My father," Fergus said, as they ambled across Ireland, where the bite of winter that in England seemed fanged, here nipped in milder fashion, "did not approve of my taking orders. He wanted to finagle me somehow into court life in London, where I was to make a name for the family."

"Your family has a good name." In any case, a known name.

"Not sufficient for my father. He wants a knighthood, and if he can't get it, he wants me to. It was a catastrophe that I was the only son. I have six sisters. My mother tells me that every time another girl was born Father went out and shot something large. A stag, most likely."

"Regrettable."

"Oh, very. He's a violent man."

I detest my father, he said to himself, but could not say the words to a man so gentle as his prior. Not for fear of shocking him—he thought that Ruthven would

159

be nearly impossible to shock. For fear of making the old monk sad, of smirching this time, this journey, with talk of the man who had sired him.

A greedy man, the son went on in his thoughts. A hard, worldly man, scornful of those weaker or poorer than he, truckling to those more powerful, better born. Pebble for his heart, stone for his conscience, stick a pin in him and gall would flow.

Until the age of eighteen he had lived in his father's world, each year unhappier in its ostentation, its wealth and comfort. Rebelling in the most emphatic way possible, he had entered the religious life and been for the first time at peace.

Now, ten years later, a professed monk, he sometimes wondered if he would ever be entirely free of the heritage of his blood. "I hope," he said, "that I have not got his temperament."

"I find no violence in your nature. Only beneficence, kindness. And," Ruthven added, remembering the abbot's words, "patience. At least, with me."

"Perhaps," said the young monk. "I sometimes feel—well, let it go."

Sometimes he felt a touch of his father's ambition, his father's cupidity. He fought against it, prayed that it should be taken from him. But it was there, a worm in the wheat.

He had entered the cloister, taken his vows, and wished no life except this, but he thought he would be obliged to spend much of it exorcising the spirit of his father, some part of whom—God grant a small part—lodged in his being, his veins.

160

He shook himself, and spoke of other things. Who knew if ever again he would leave the monastery, or have for company a man so altogether *good*—he had no other word for it—as Prior Ruthven.

"I wish you didn't have to die," he said, as they passed a field already touched with the green of spring. Or, he added to himself, if you must die, I wish you'd come back, like the spring.

He could not say a thing like that aloud.

Ruthven smiled. "And you—would you wish to remain forever on this earth? Never see Heaven?"

"Oh, no!" Fergus exclaimed.

"Then please—do not be after wishing such a fate on me."

They rode for several miles in silence before Ruthven spoke again.

"They have, at Ballyvaghan, a fine library, Fergus. You will take pleasure in that. The monks of Ireland, during the dark centuries of pillage and destruction that took place over the rest of the world, lived in comparative peace. Oh, they suffered raids, too, as savage as any others. But not so frequent. And they made books—such books—"

"I've seen some of them, Prior Ruthven. In our own abbey library, and at Canterbury. And once I went on a pilgrimage to the Isle of Lindisfarne, to see the great Gospel books. Oh, they are beautiful beyond words to describe. Do you know, Father, that the Lindisfarne Gospels were written and illuminated perhaps four, maybe even five, centuries ago? I can see it still—the picture of Saint John enthroned. The colors, the colors! The expression of the saint, looking from the page, as if right at me...."

Dropping the reins to Jackstraw's neck, he put his hands to his lips and rode for a distance with eyes closed.

Ruthven made no move to break the silence.

"It was because of those books," Fergus at length continued, "that I became a scribe. One day, God willing, I shall myself make a book. Not a copy. A book of my own, and I shall illuminate it, too...." He drew a deep breath. "Abbot Brendan says we can thank and bless the Irish monks for preserving—what did he call it?—the humane part of human nature. The part that loves scholarship and art. How wonderful, that you are Irish."

Ruthven held up a gently quelling hand. "God's will, Fergus. God's will."

But he, too, thought it wonderful.

On the seventh day from the morning they had left, the two monks came to the abbey of Ballyvaghan, and were there enfolded, Fergus with hospitality, Ruthven with love and tenderness.

"We give thanks to God that you made it back to us," said the abbot. He was nearly as old as Ruthven and had never seen him before. "We are overjoyed that you made it home."

"I never doubted that I would," Ruthven said.

CHAPTER XVI

ERGUS," Prior Ruthven said from his bed in the abbot's quarters. "I shall be sorry indeed to see the last of you, but your task, so faithfully done, is over." At Fergus's uncomprehending look, he added, "You must start back for Cerne."

"Right away?"

"Today."

"But Ruthven—I mean, Father—I haven't had a chance to *see* anything."

"You have been to the chapel of Saint Cirian in the church. Abbot Padraic tells me he let you touch the reliquary."

"Oh, *yes*," said the young monk, catching his breath.

"And how did it—what were your sensations?"

163

"I can't describe them, Father."

"No, of course not. I shouldn't have asked."

Fergus stood at the prior's bedside, recalling the moment when Abbot Padraic had drawn aside the curtain that shrouded the reliquary. For a moment he had been disappointed. A leather casket, where he'd expected gold, or anyway chased bronze or silver. The leather cracked and dull, the gems few and not fine. Yet, in a moment more he knew that this was how a saint would wish his relics housed . . . without adornment or show of wealth.

He had asked the abbot how it came that the claim of the contents was so specific. "I do not doubt—oh, not in any way—that the saint's lock of hair and the bit of his fingernail lie here within. But I wonder how— what the history of it is."

"The casket," Abbot Padraic explained, "was discovered in the souterrain of an ancient castle, sacked by Danish pirates. Within was a parchment page, written in Irish, that set forth the circumstances. The monks of the abbey, in fear for their holy treasures rather than for their lives, I make no doubt, took refuge in the castle—for all the good it did them—and cached what they could in this souterrain."

"Where was the castle?"

"It lies less than a mile from this, in ruins. Our own abbey was not founded then, but there was a small one, atop a cliff, also close by and also long since in ruins. As there is no evidence of another cloister for many miles, we assume that the contents of the

164

souterrain came from there. The reliquary casket, and some altar furnishings—now on our own altar—were somehow overlooked by the Viking raiders. Well, it stands to reason that pillage and ransack as they would, they could not uncover everything hidden against their coming."

"Was anything else found?"

The abbot looked unhappy. "Yes. There was evidence of a considerable library, impossible to restore. Just a mass of vellum and parchment, chewed by rats, eroded by damp. Impossible even to assess how many volumes comprised the whole, for when we made an attempt to move them, the entire collection fell apart."

"Oh, awful. Terrible," said Fergus, shaken with regret for the loss of books he'd not heard of till this moment. "Think how much was lost—how much of learning, and beauty, and—and the work of hands."

"I try not to think of it. But the mind goes its way, and I feel bitterly deprived."

"Your library here is a fine one," Fergus said.

"Still, we always mourn the lost lamb." Abbot Padraic brooded a moment, then told Fergus that Prior Ruthven had been asking for him.

Raised by his father to consider the Irish still on the near side of savagery, everything about this abbey— its church, its guesthouse and other buildings, its beautiful grounds and gardens, its fields now winter bare but surely glorious come springtime—had surprised Fergus.

"Why, it's as fine as Cerne," he'd blurted when he and Prior Ruthven first spied it, then flushed with annoyance at himself.

Now he was being told to start for England after but one night at Ballyvaghan.

"Prior Ruthven," he said humbly. "Please—give me a day or two more. I may never be in Ireland again. Let me ride out by myself and see the countryside, and meditate alone. Abbot Padraic says I can take one of the horses—I haven't been on a fine horse for so long. And these Irish horses—"

"You wish to remain in order to ride a horse?"

"Even a monk has wants," Fergus said in a low voice. And to himself—no, a monk should not want, merely wait.

Prior Ruthven, motionless under a soft woolen blanket, said in a voice grown faint, "You have been a good companion, Fergus. I give thanks for your strength and your patience. I do not think Abbot Brendan will grudge you an extra day. Just one. Then you must go."

Fergus knelt at the bedside, felt the old thin hand on his head, murmured thanks, received his prior's blessing. He tried to withdraw reluctantly, but once out of the room ran to the stables, where an ostler saddled for him a great black gelding that pranced and tossed its head as Fergus mounted.

"Castor, his name is," said the stableman. "He's the spirit of a stallion to him, Brother. The kind that's after testing his rider, so."

"We'll get along fine," said Fergus over his shoulder

as he and Castor set off eagerly for the abbey gate, and out onto the road.

"Oh, these Irish horses!" he cried aloud in wild elation, and wondered if there were horses in Heaven. His father had several mounts, but ah, none so fine as this.

Taking great gulps of air, watching his breath and Castor's fly about mistily, he set the horse to a canter. Over a field they flew, then down a lane for nearly a mile before he reined in and settled to a trot again. He wanted to see, to take into his mind, into his heart, a picture of this land that would remain his forever.

It was a day so clear, so coldly sunny, that he thought if he flicked his finger against the air it would chime like one of Abbot Brendan's wineglasses.

Suddenly—looking about to be sure no one was close—he gave a shout of exultation and put Castor to a gallop.

In another mile, he brought the horse down to a canter, a trot, a walk. Patting the smoothly muscled neck, he leaned over and whispered in a backward flicking ear, "You're the grand fellow altogether, you are, and I wish I could steal you home with me, you Irish beauty."

Smiling contentedly, he began to look about. He was near a cliff that rose straight from the road for what seemed several hundred feet. There were steps cut in the rock. Leaning backward, he could descry a wall, obviously ancient but still in good condition. Behind it must be the abbey ruin that Abbot Padraic had spoken of.

167

"See here, Castor," he said, dismounting. "I trust you altogether, but just in case you should take a fancy to go home without me, you won't mind if I tether you to this tree for a space, while I climb up yonder and see what's to be seen?"

Castor whinnied, a horse accustomed to explanations.

Climbing the steep rock face, Fergus emerged on a plateau that overlooked the ocean.

There it was. The remains of what had been a small monastic community, centuries ago. The stones of the surrounding wall and of the cloister buildings were scattered, yet some kept their ancient place. Timbers burned. Bell tower collapsed.

Abbot Padraic had said that after previous Viking raids, both castle and abbey had been rebuilt, but apparently the last invasion—there had been none since—proved so devastating, in every way, that no effort of renewal was considered.

Or perhaps, thought Fergus, there had been no survivors, monk or warrior, to undertake the great task.

He walked slowly down the roofless church nave. Stone steps curved up to a vanished pulpit. Storms, driving in through broken windows, had left debris— branches, sand, rotted leaves covered the floor.

He left the church and entered what had probably been the refectory, also open to the air. He could make out, on the east wall, a faded painting of Christ on the cross. Next was the lavatorium, a rainwater cistern above it long since fallen to rubble. In the stone trough lay a dead bird.

Leaving the wrecked abbey buildings, he crossed a rock-strewn pasture, and came to the cliff's edge, thinking of the monks who had once lived and worked and died on this hill, some peacefully, no doubt, some at the hands of marauding Danes.

Had they been taken by surprise? No. If Abbot Padraic was right, and surely he must be, the treasures of the castle souterrain had been taken from here and hidden there.

So they had had time to escape. Time, even, for a scribe to write on parchment a message to the future, and enclose it with the sacred relics.

He glanced eastward. There on a distant eminence stood what remained of the castle. Filled with ruins, this country was. Everywhere the remnants of small beehive chapels, little windowless stone churches, and slightly larger monasteries, such as this. Far smaller than any known today, it could have housed but few monks. Yet these had been among the learned Irish religious who wrote books, and illuminated them, and preserved, as Abbot Brendan had once said, the humane portion of human nature.

How the world should grieve for the lost volumes, hidden against discovery, destroyed by time.

He walked to the edge of the cliff. Seabirds clung to the cliffside, raucous and quarrelsome. No nests now, but what a winged nursery it would be, in a few weeks' time.

I wish I could be here, he thought, when the spring comes.

For a long time he remained, looking out to sea,

trying to will himself into the mind, the spirit, of a monk, now dust, who had stood just so, drawing breath, alive as he was himself this moment, and seen this same restless ocean ride in and break upon the rocks below.

It was possible that a man like himself had stood where he stood now and had seen, in a cursed armada, the sails of the Vikings loom over the horizon.

Descending the steps, he mounted Castor, and turned toward the abbey.

At a small overgrown path he'd not noticed when galloping past, he paused. In a moment, as if drawn, as if *directed*, he started into the brush, found that the undergrowth, the hanging branches, would be too thick and chancy for a horse.

"Just this one time more," he said.

Tethering Castor to the slender trunk of a hornbeam tree, he walked down the woodsy lane, past a deserted mill with a broken waterwheel that the brook still coursed over. Pushing still deeper, hoping he would not get lost but filled with strange determination, he came at length to a spot so overgrown that only with an axe could he go farther.

He sat on a stone to meditate, to pray a little, giving thanks for the trip with Prior Ruthven, for this day of unmerited and joyous freedom.

For no reason he could ever afterward explain, he picked up a small branch and began to poke about, lifting aside plants that trailed over the rock he sat on, then idly pushing away stones that seemed to be piled against it.

For no better reason than he'd picked it up, he tossed the branch aside, rose, glanced down, and saw that he'd laid open what might once have been a vixen's den, a badger set. A deep hole, long unoccupied by any beast.

But how, he wondered, so covertly disguised? No fox, no badger had put these stones against the entrance, or pulled plants across so as to hide it. Getting to his knees, he thrust his hand into the hole, and encountered—something.

He jerked back in alarm, leaned forward again, clutched whatever it was in a strong grip, and dragged a bundle out of this lair.

Sitting back on his heels, hand to his mouth, he gaped in wonder.

What had he found?

A dirt-encrusted, moldy, hide-wrapped package. Something hidden, sometime, by someone—and he, Fergus, had been led to it, as to the Grail.

Trembling, he stretched forth a tentative finger, hesitated, then threw back the cowhide. It fell apart in rotted shreds, revealing a large banded tin box. Taking the stout knife he carried with him, he pried for several minutes at the rusted hinges, turned back the lid and gazed within. More wrappings, but these in good condition, carefully sewn.

Looking all around, though no living thing was near except a flock of rooks circling and calling above the trees, Fergus cautiously undid the laces, undid the wrappings, looked for a long time at what was revealed, then covered his face with his hands.

"Please, God...please God...help me..."

He did not know what he was saying, what asking. He realized too well what he was feeling—a shuddering ecstasy that in a recess of his mind he recognized as sinfully physical.

Here, under his eyes, lying where he could put his *hands* on it, was a book. A book no other eyes had seen for—for how long? Someone, a monk—surely he who had made this—had secreted it in the deep woods, in the deep hole, against discovery by pirates. Had he hoped that one day it would be found in its place of concealment? Hoped that it would be treated with reverent understanding—that one day it would be given asylum?

There was a title page.

A History of Saint Patrick of Ireland.

The hand looked like the minuscule cursive he'd seen on the parchment page in the reliquary casket. The capitals were already drawn, but not painted. After the title page, a carpet page most brilliantly illuminated, the inks and paints hardly faded.

Again and again Fergus put a finger forward, repeatedly withdrew it. He was afraid to touch something so sacred. And yet—he alone had been led to find it. It was his discovery, and none other's.

His should be the first touch upon it.

Why should he scruple to turn the pages with

reverent fingers? Whoever made this intended for it to be seen. Fergus *knew* that. One day, when he had written his own book, for God first of course, but after that for the joy of giving something of beauty and learning to the world, he would want it to be seen.

And touched. Touched! Such a book called for the hand of man upon it.

"Whoever you are," he said, looking upward through tightly budded branches, "whoever you were ... you must have wanted me to find this, wanted me to see the work of your hands, to put into *my* hands this book you created. Else why have you led me here?"

That he had been led he did not doubt.

His heart seemed to fly about and beat against his ribs as he crouched and picked the volume up in hands that shook.

Tenderly, tenderly he examined the volume. A history of Saint Patrick, in Latin, the text complete, the illuminations unfinished. But oh, the blessed radiance of the pages the long-dead monk had brought to completion!

Fergus had seen manuscripts more polished, written with a finer hand. But in this volume that had lain so long hidden there was something endearingly crude, a youthful beauty *sui generis*—that transcended what he had looked upon before.

"And waiting for me," Fergus said aloud. "For me!"

It was growing dark, and he must get back to the abbey.

But he lingered still. Carefully laying back the carpet page, he came upon a poem. A poem! The page entirely decorated, with a vine trailing down from the initial, aflutter with birds and insects and blossoms. Who wrote this poem? Who lettered and painted so wondrous a thing?

Leaning close, he made out the words *Cormac me fecit.*

"Cormac made me," said the exultant young monk. "And *Fergus me revelit!*"

Fergus unveiled me!

He could not read the verse itself, written in Irish.

Wrapping the volume with infinite care, he replaced it in the tin box, tried to wrap the outer, rotting hide around it but could not. Well, it would be here only another day now.

Tomorrow he would take leave of Prior Ruthven, of Abbot Padraic. He would mount Jackstraw and return here. The tin box would fit in his saddlebag and he would carry his treasure back to Cerne. No one here would miss it. How could they, not knowing of its existence so close to them all these years?

"No," he said, mounting Castor, "I found it. It is mine. Or," he added, making a grasp at self-denial and humility, "it belongs to England, and to Cerne. Since *I* found it," he repeated.

CHAPTER XVII

ERGUS AND HIS abbot walked the cloister, after Sext, cowls down, hands deep in their sleeves. Passing brothers glanced at them curiously.

"Gone a long time, Brother Fergus was," said a novice.

"Too long," said another. "Even to get to the west of Ireland and back. Fancies himself."

"Perhaps Prior Ruthven died, and he waited for the interment?"

"We'd have heard."

They encountered the eye of the novice master and fell silent. Which does not, thought the one, prevent a person from thinking that Brother Fergus is not yet mantled in humility.

"Takes liberties, that one," he whispered to his

175

companion, who shook his head, not disagreeing, but aware still of the novice master's regard.

"So you took leave of your hosts," the abbot was saying in a level tone, "not telling Abbot Padraic, or your prior, what you had discovered in their woods."

"I couldn't tell Prior Ruthven," Fergus exclaimed, looked about and lowered his voice. "He would have made me *leave* it."

"Just so."

"Besides, Father Abbot—who can say for sure that those were their own woods—"

"We might assume it. But go on. You took your leave, mounted Jackstraw, returned to the cache, and concealed the volume in your saddlebag."

"Not concealed," Fergus said sulkily. "Put it in. Where else would I carry it?"

"And then?"

That day it had been snowing lightly. He'd gone for miles, almost the entire morning, on plodding Jackstraw, with the sacred volume in his saddlebag, when all at once, unbidden, unwelcome, he heard his father's voice.

"Fergus, you are in possession of a treasure of untold value, which you should bring to me as I am your father who gave you life and *I want that book*! Think! Fergus, think! I could present it to King Henry. If that didn't bring a knighthood falling into my hands, apples don't drop from trees."

Fergus had halted in the road, the snow falling ever

more thickly. The prospect of the return ride, even more than of having to confess his action, was daunting. Almost terrifying.

And yet—

Always he had feared that something of his father's cupidity remained in him, something of the hard ambition that dismembered the rights of others.

Putting his hand on Jackstraw's rough neck, he'd murmured, "I do not have a right to this book. Taking it back to Cerne, saying it was for the glory of the abbey—words, only words."

He wanted it to be where he could see it, read it. *Touch* it. Have it by him, always. To part with it would be painful almost past endurance. Yet he had known, almost from the moment he put the volume in his saddlebag, that he would not be able to keep it.

"Ah well, Jackstraw," he'd said aloud, in a cracked and grieving voice, "back we go." Lifting the reins to turn the mule's head, he'd faced into the whirling snow and gone westward again.

When a second tour of the cloister was completed, Abbot Brendan said, "Am I to know, Fergus, why you changed your mind about bringing the book to us?"

"I guess I decided I was stealing it."

"Not surprising, since that's what you were doing."

Even now, Fergus felt a stir of protest. Who, after all, had found—

"Father Abbot," he exclaimed, "I am bemired! I do not know what I am, what impulses are in me. I walk here with you, and remember Prior Ruthven's face

177

when I returned and showed him the book, and how Abbot Padraic did not say one word of rebuke, and I do not know what I feel." He sighed. "Except unworthy. Most wormlike and unworthy."

"You go from extreme to extreme, Fergus. From pride to groveling self-abasement. In time you'll find a middle course. Meanwhile, take into account that you did turn back, you did confess your transgression."

"I must do penance."

"We shall see."

"I *wish* a hard penance!"

"Very well, Fergus. I'll set you one, if you cannot feel that you've sufficiently repented." He smiled. "But, for now, my son, let us go to the library and look again upon the page that Abbot Padraic sent to Cerne as a gift. A thing of such beauty, and so—gently personal. A treasure, indeed."

"I can scarcely believe yet that it is here, that they gave it me to take to you."

"Oh, I can believe it. As they said—rightly—but for you, the volume would most likely never have been discovered."

When he had returned to Ballyvaghan and proffered the holy volume to Abbot Padraic, explaining in a tear-shaken voice how he had found and made off with it, the abbot had looked at him for a long time without speaking.

At length, he'd said, "We'll take it to Prior Ruthven. He should be the first to see it. The first, that is, after yourself." He had sounded, to Fergus's almost fright-

178

ened astonishment, in no way reproachful, only matter-of-fact.

In the prior's bedroom, they propped Ruthven against pillows, and laid the book—so light to hold, for all its value, its sacred import—on his lap. The old prior turned the folio pages slowly, gazed at them with wondering eyes.

He looked at Fergus, who stood with bowed head near the door. "I can see how you were tempted, Brother Fergus. I might have been, myself."

But, of course, he would not have been. Nor would Abbot Padraic, or Abbot Brendan. Or, Fergus supposed wretchedly, most of his brother monks.

"Unworthy, unworthy," he'd whispered. *Mea culpa, mea culpa.*

"Yes," said Abbot Padraic. "It was a grave fault. But you reconsidered. That atones for much."

Fergus thought not, but was grateful for the abbot's words, even more thankful to be told to go to the chapel of Saint Cirian and pray. He was overwhelmed with emotion, with repentance and—there it was, still in him!—with passionate regret that he would never see the book again.

The road grows stonier, the way grows steeper, he'd been thinking as Abbot Padraic said, "You will have to spend another night here. We shan't put you out in this storm."

"Thank you," Fergus said wearily. Under snug roof or snowy sky didn't seem to matter.

He spent the night in vigil in the chapel of Saint Cirian.

179

On the following morning, he was called into Ruthven's room again, where he found the abbot and the prior looking pleased, smiling upon him as on a favored son.

"Fergus," said Prior Ruthven. "You are at once too proud and too contrite. Full of self. Self-regard and self-reproach. Abbot Brendan and I have prayed that your steps will find a more modest path. Yesterday, I believe you set your foot in that direction."

Fergus bowed his head.

"Come, come, my son. These are not words of rebuke. Perhaps just a last word of counsel, as we shall not meet again? Take it as meant. And now, Abbot Padraic and I have a gift for you. That is—for the abbey at Cerne."

"A gift?"

"Yes. One that will give you—and all at Cerne—great joy. Look—" He gestured toward the blanket where lay a page of the volume. "Did you have a chance, hurried as you must have been, to read this?"

Fergus approached the bed, looked down. It was the poem.

Four stanzas, most elaborately, exquisitely illuminated, and written in—"I cannot read the language," he said softly. "I have only Latin, besides my own tongue. I read *Cormac me fecit*, but nothing more."

"It's Irish," said Abbot Padraic. "A little poem written centuries ago to the cat who is lying asleep, as you see, in the initial letter. There can be no doubt of the model. I see the monk—I do not see him young or old, just a brother like ourselves—working at his book, his eye lighting on his cat—or, I suppose, the abbey cat—and in my mind he is moved to pen a verse to this companion of his silence. I find it almost more touching than the history of Saint Patrick itself."

Fergus looked from one priest to the other. "You mean for me to have it? I mean, to take it back to Cerne. As a gift? For us to keep?"

"We think, Fergus, you have earned it. Who knows if this holy book would ever have been uncovered at all, save for your curiosity?"

Save for my being led there by a monk's vanished hand, thought Fergus, but he said, "Abbot Padraic. Would you read it me?"

"With infinite pleasure. One of the brothers, last night, copied it out in Latin for you and your brothers at Cerne. But I shall read it with joy. First, so that you may hear our tongue, in Irish. Then in Latin."

Now, back at Cerne, in the library, with the sun lying in swaths across the great carved cherry table where Abbot Brendan had put the folio page for all the brethren to see later in the day, he and Fergus, without touching, leaned over it reverently, to examine each flowery detail, each leaf of ivy, each nesting bird, each careful and graceful minuscule letter.

They looked at the white cat asleep at the foot of the blossoming initial letter, *I*.

Neither could read the Irish script, but Abbot Brendan, who already had the Latin by heart, recited softly . . .

I, and Pangur Ban my cat
'Tis a like task we are at:
Hunting mice is his delight,
Hunting words I sit all night. . . .

The monk who wrote it is a long time dead, lost to any memory, thought Fergus. He can never be summoned up. But here is Pangur Ban, this cat, a gift to the world. Because that monk wrote of him. *Because I found him.*

He experienced a flash of exultant self-delight before firmly turning his eyes and his feet toward the modest, selfless path he meant to tread from now on, yet hesitated a moment longer, thinking:

There is no reason why even the humblest, the most self-regardless of monks should not—*write a book.*

So in peace our task we ply,
Pangur Ban, my cat and I:
In our arts we find our bliss,
I have mine and he has his.